Why Me?

By

Robert Kawka

Bob Kawka

Copyright © 2025

All Rights Reserved

ISBN: 978-1-966642-60-2

Dedication

iii

To all those who believe we are not alone.

Acknowledgment

I acknowledge the countless hours of proofreading and listening to my wild ideas that my wife, Elaine, gave to this story, and Shaina, at New York Publishers, for patiently guiding me through the difference between academic publishing and "real-world" publishing.

Table of Contents

About the Author

Bob retired from a fulfilling career teaching special needs students in 2002. He now lives with his wife, Elaine, in Port Orange, Florida. In retirement, Bob enjoys writing and dedicates his time to crafting custom pens, combining creativity with craftsmanship in each unique piece.

Chapter 1

"You ready, Dear?" said Mary as she packed the large cloth shopping bag. "You know that the concert starts at the Farmer's Market around seven, and I want to look for some of those special Hawaiian onions for this new recipe."

"I'm coming," said Tom, hurriedly tying his last shoelace.

"I'll be in the car. You lock up," said Mary, trying to hurry Tom along without being too obvious.

"OK," said Tom, aware of Mary's ploy learned over the last 30 years of a wonderful marriage producing one son, a college graduate who was doing quite well as a geologist. The ride over was the usual drive down Euclid Avenue and under the freeway with the usual comments about the new Junior College construction next to the freeway.

"I wonder when they will be ready for business," said Mary as they sailed by the construction at the awesome speed of 35 miles per hour.

"You know you might want to see if they are hiring part-time instructors. That way, you could pick up some extra money for that work you want to do on your boat," said Mary, referring to the family's 20-year-old Glastron outboard that Tom would putter around in for hours as a diversion to his teaching job at the local elementary school.

"Pull in there," Mary said, spotting a choice parking place near where she wanted to go shopping at the local Tuesday night Farmers Market. Of the surrounding farmers' market, the one in downtown Ontario, California, was her favorite.

Mary was looking forward to trying out a new recipe on Tom that she had seen demonstrated on a Food TV show and had gotten the recipe from the internet. This was to be a surprise for Tom's birthday this weekend.

They parked the car and got the onions and some special Jalapeno Olive Oil at one of the produce stands that Tom spotted during their stroll around the market. After they had returned to the car with their "swag," as Mary called it, they walked hand-in-hand over to the newly dedicated gazebo where a local band was just starting to play some real music, not that noise that kids call music nowadays, but real music from the mid-50s' and 60s.'

'Life,' thought Tom, 'couldn't get any better. Here I am, about ready to retire with my wonderful wife of 29 years.

Why me?

Actually, catching up on some fishing, travel, and in general, having some personal fun after devoting one-half of our lives to educating other people's children.'

Mary was a teacher at a local high school, and they planned to retire together.

The music started. Tom put his hand around Mary's waist, and they started swaying to the wonderful music.

'This is great,' thought Tom. 'Now, if they could only stop those noisy planes from the nearby Ontario airport from messing up the concert, it would be even better. The worst offenders were those noisy helicopters. Speaking of which, it sounded like about 300 of those loud sounding copters were going to pass right over the concert. Oh, well, so much for the joys of civilization.'

Speaking of the joys of civilization, why was his cell phone ringing? Only three people had his number. Mary, who was standing beside him, and the kids whom they had talked with earlier that day.

"Are you going to answer that thing, Mr. Technology person?" jibed Mary with a grin.

Tom fumbled the thing out, thinking how many times he had complained about other people's noisy phones, and here he was making almost as much racket as those damn helicopters.

He pressed the receive button and said, "Hello."

Mary, watching him out of the corner of her eye, thought he was having a heart attack. His face got red, and he was almost yelling into the phone, something about "not now" or "what are you talking about?"

She couldn't hear him because those helicopters were almost directly overhead and were too low, plus they were shining lights over the crowd like the police copters occasionally do to show off.

Tom turned to her, handed her the car keys, and said in a very hoarse voice, "You'll have to take the car home. It seems that I've got something to attend to, and I will call you later."

"Is everything OK?"

"Yes, but due to some bureaucratic mistake, I've got to go!"

"But where?" said Mary.

Why me?

"There," said Tom, giving her a quick peck on the cheek and pointing to the big military-type chopper just landing on a grassy knoll across from them.

Two other choppers were circling, illuminating the area with powerful spotlights. People were scattering from the powerful downdraft from the rotors. As Tom approached it, the door opened, and three people got out. Two immediately spread out from the doorway carrying some sort of automatic weapons and looking as if they would like to use them. The third person appeared to be in charge. Mary couldn't tell his rank because he was too far away to clearly see, but he was in a blue Air Force uniform, and when Tom approached, he saluted Tom, who appeared to return his salute. Tom got into the chopper. It took off, and that was the last Mary saw of Tom for almost five months.

Chapter 2

Once aboard the big military chopper, Tom was efficiently escorted to a seat, strapped in, and large headphones were placed over his ears.

"What the hell is this all about?" said Tom as the chopper lifted off, almost leaving his stomach behind.

A voice on his cell phone had said, "Your name is Tom Roberts. You have a wife named Mary and a son who graduated from State. You are being activated under Project Pyramid. For the sake of your country, wife, and your son, please get on the chopper that just landed. If not, your lives will be in danger. This is not a joke, but for real. We can discuss your part in it soon, but you must get on that chopper now!"

The voice on the phone sounded familiar, but Tom couldn't quite place it. He remembered saying, "Why me?"

And the voice said, "It will be explained to you shortly, but you must get on the chopper now!"

The Man who saluted him as he approached the chopper was a major one, and what was more surprising was the way Tom automatically returned the salute.

Why me?

Once the chopper stopped ascending like a rocket-powered elevator, Tom turned to the officer and said, "What the hell is this all about, and why am I here?"

"Sir, my orders were to pick you up one way or another and get you to the airport and put you on that jet over there," said the officer, pointing out a window to a Gulf Stream executive jet sitting on the general aviation side of Ontario International Airport, which was only 4 miles from downtown Ontario.

Almost before the officer finished explaining, they landed right next to the jet, and the major hustled Tom out and up the stairs of the business jet, whose engines were already turning over.

Aboard the taxiing jet, Tom was strapped into a luxurious leather seat by a very attentive young lady wearing sergeant's stripes.

"Young lady, do you know what this is all about? Or at least do you know where we're headed?"

"No, sir. All I know is that you are very important because we were diverted from a VIP flight to Hawaii to pick you up."

"We just left two congressmen and their staffs at this airport to take you where you are going, wherever that is," added the sergeant.

As they rapidly climbed to cruising altitude, the sergeant told Tom he could walk around, showed him where the head was, and advised him to take advantage of some of the best food he had had in quite a while.

'So, this is how congressmen are treated on junkets,' thought Tom, munching on a croissant black forest ham sandwich.

About the time that Tom was starting his second sandwich, the pilot, a full colonel, came back and introduced himself as Colonel Nickerson.

"I don't know who you are, and I don't want to know, but I just wanted to shake hands with a person who can bump two house appropriations senators."

"Well, Colonel, if it's any consolation to you, I don't know who that person is either. I'm just a schoolteacher from California. Perhaps it would help to know where we are going. Where are we going?"

"Well, sir, we are getting that information as we speak. Because of the nature of this flight, we would not be given any info until we were on a heading of 90 degrees at an altitude of 18000 feet. We are there, and the information is being dumped into our flight computer right now."

The phone beside Tom began to chime slightly, and Nickerson answered, "Yes," paused and said, "OK." He turned to Tom and said, "Sir, I guess you had better strap yourself in, as it seems we are starting our descent."

"Descent to where?" said Tom." "Hell, if I know," said Nickerson as he turned and walked back to the flight deck.

Chapter 3

'The descent into "hell" went very smoothly. They let down over a small city, probably somewhere in the California Desert,' thought Tom, 'since they hadn't been airborne very long.'

The landing was so smooth that Tom wasn't really sure when the wheels actually touched the ground. They taxied up to a poorly lit, low-slung building that appeared to be deserted or abandoned. The young sergeant directed Tom to the building.

"Now, what do I do?" asked Tom.

"I don't know," said the sergeant.

"But, let me check." She lifted a cell phone and punched a number. "Sir, what does our passenger do now?" She paused, shaking her head several times as if subconsciously answering some question asked on the phone. She put it down, smiled a stewardess smile, and said, "You are to wait in the office here, and someone will fetch you."

"There's obviously no one there," said Tom, stating the obvious.

"Sir, our orders are to deliver you to this spot, then return and pick up the congressmen and continue our trip. I would assume that someone will be by shortly since someone has gone through a lot of trouble getting you here. However, why don't you take a couple of sandwiches and this thermos of coffee since there doesn't look to be a restaurant nearby," she said, handing him a thermos and a small bag of sandwiches she had been carrying.

She was so smooth that Tom didn't realize that he had been effectively and efficiently escorted out the door of the plane and was headed down the stairs before he knew it.

Tom barely reached the stairs to the building before the engines were revving up, and the plane began to taxi.

Tom got to the building, turned, and looked at the departing plane. He thought he caught a salute from the pilot's side but wasn't sure in the dark.

The plane quickly taxied out the short distance to the single active runway, turned, and took off in about the time it took to tell about it.

Suddenly, it was very quiet. It was so quiet that Tom could hear the crickets, the coyotes, and even the lone drink machine sitting just outside the door of the building.

Also, Tom could not see any living person in any direction. Inside, there was a counter and two old leather chairs.

'No doubt for visiting VIPs,' thought Tom. The other side of the counter contained an old beat-up wooden desk, 'Like my first desk at school many years ago,' thought Tom, smiling at the pleasant remembering of his first day as a teacher and how intimidated he felt at the sight of 36 fifth graders all waiting for him to do something after he had called roll… twice because he was so nervous he forgot he had called it already.

"But enough of that, let's see if we can find a phone," he said to himself.

Three seconds later, he discovered that there were no phones in this part of the world, at least none that he could see.

'Well, Mr. Technology, what about your cell phone?' he thought.

"I am getting old, but I have been through some very unusual activities, so I just had a few distractions," he said, mentally cutting himself some slack for his forgetfulness. When he tried his cell, the battery was dead. "Damn!"   he thought. "So much for modern technology when a cell cannot keep a charge for longer than a couple of hours." He would later find out that the sweet young sergeant was a senior field agent for the NSA and, while he was eating, scanned him for weapons, cameras, and communication or tracking devices, all of which she would disable. That was why he would also find that he had lost his favorite pocketknife during the hustle and bustle of the trip.

Ten minutes later, Tom had explored every nook and cranny in the building, found the men's room, and walked around the outside of the small building. He had just decided that he would wait until light and then try to find a way into town or at least find a phone and get Mary to pick him up, assuming he could find out where this place was. He settled himself into one of the old leather chairs and found it to be surprisingly comfortable (not realizing that the design and artificial aging of that chair cost taxpayers almost as much as his first car). He had just taken a big bite out of one of those delicious sandwiches packed by the sergeant when he saw a car pull up to the building. After carefully rewrapping the sandwich, "just in case," he got up and walked to the front door, where he saw the oldest yellow cab he had ever seen. There was no design to it; it was just a big box on wheels, and it was dirty. Tom's impression was that the taxi had reached the theoretical limits of acquiring dirt. It couldn't possibly hold any more dirt than the dirt that somehow managed to stick to the faded yellow paint. Tom asked the driver if he was for hire, figuring he could at least get a ride into town, but the Man said in broken English that he was already hired. He was supposed to pick up a Mister Tom Roberts. "That's me," said Tom. "Prove it," said the driver, apparently not one to mince words. Tom dutifully showed his driver's license. "You got any luggage? That's extra," said the driver. "No," said Tom. "Then get in, time's money, and the meter's running," said the driver. Tom tried to get in on the passenger's side but found the door locked. "You get in the back. I don't let people sit up front," grunted the driver, who was waving a hand at the back.

Once he was seated in the back, the driver warned Tom to keep the windows closed since there would be a lot of dust.

Tom would later learn that the heavy tinting would effectively keep him from seeing out as well as keep any observers from seeing in. The driver jammed the car into gear and took off.

Tom wondered if there was an ejection seat for him since they were obviously flying and would undoubtedly crash in the next few minutes, if not sooner.

After ten minutes of the twisty and turning roads, Tom was hopelessly disoriented. And when they pulled up in front of a hacienda-styled ranch-like building twenty minutes later, he knew that he would never be able to find his way back.

On the front porch sat the ugliest, oldest Mexican Tom had ever seen.

"You the new guy?" yelled the Mexican.

"I guess so," said Tom, who had tried to get out of the car as soon as it slowed enough for him to do so but found the door locked.

The driver looked back and explained, 'That was to make sure passengers paid their fares before leaving. But yours is already paid so that I can let you out.' Tom thought, 'I'm not getting back in there with that driver ever, even if it means I have to walk back. Besides not being able to drive, he's crazy!'

Tom later learned that Bill, the driver, was trained at the Bob Bondurant School of Racing and at the State

Department's special driving school outside of Washington, where they train very special drivers to protect high-ranking government officials at cabinet level and above. The washout rate is about 90% during the 6-week course, which covers everything from driving in suburban ghettos to off-road challenges in a 4-wheel drive vehicle.

Tom's driver was first in his class, and his scores still haven't been topped.

"Hey, Senora, who's going to pay for this?" yelled the driver at the Mexican on the porch.

"You, thieving Mexican, you have been paid and tipped. Now get out of here afore I clean your ears with my baby here," yelled the Mexican on the porch, lifting what looked like a baseball bat and pointing it at the driver.

"OK," yelled the driver. "I'm just trying to make up for all the times you cheated me."

"Vamoose," yelled the Mexican on the porch, who was now standing up and coming down the stairs.

"OK, OK!" said the driver, putting the car in gear and pulling away in a cloud of dust that promptly settled over Tom, causing a brief fit of coughing.

"Don't just stand there, come on in!" yelled the Mexican on the porch.

"Where is this?" said Tom.

"Come on in, and it will be explained," said the Mexican who had suddenly lost his accent and who now was standing beside Tom, gently but firmly guiding him up the steps and through the door.

Inside the front room was what you would expect to find in a dude ranch. Comfortable-looking couches, a big fireplace, nice chairs and tables, and a few cheap reproductions on the walls depicting stylized cowboy life in the old West. In fact, the most striking feature of the whole place was the woman sitting at a table doing some writing.

She looked up, and Tom looked into eyes that seemed to suck him into her. Those eyes stared at him, surrounded by a frame of long brown hair falling to breast height. She got up, and he was easily able to imagine the kind of figure that had attracted him to Mary. She was athletic, firm, and very obviously a woman, even in the full dress and bolero she was wearing.

"You poor thing," she said, walking over and patting him on the arm, raising a small cloud of dust. "I see Bill was having his fun. I shall have to talk to him about treating guests this way. I'm sure you must feel the need to wash and rest, so please follow me, and we will take care of you."

Tom said, "Where are we? Can I call my wife and let her know I'm OK?"

"That all has been attended to. We are in California," she said as she escorted him through the door at the back of the room. In the next room, Tom's mouth actually dropped open. He was in a very modern reception area that any high-tech company would have been proud to claim.

Seated at the reception desk sat a secretary in Air Force blues wearing first lieutenant's silver bars.

"Welcome to Project Pyramid, sir."

Chapter 4

"What the hell is this all about?" said Tom when he had recovered from his shock at seeing the room. "Why am I here?" Before he could say anything more, the woman said, "Tom, all your questions will be answered shortly. But first, there are a few simple formalities for you to go through. And once you've signed in and cleaned up, Dr. Kafka will explain the whole thing to you."

"Sir, if you will, please sign our guest book here," said the Lieutenant, handing Tom a pen and pointing to a blank line. Tom signed in, and then the Lieutenant pointed to a plate on his desk and asked Tom to put his right hand on the plate. When Tom did, a light came on and scanned his hand. "Please state your first and last name and your social security number."

After Tom had finished logging in, the woman turned to him. "My name is Ruth, Dr. Ruth Thompson, and no, I'm not related in any way to another Dr. Ruth whom you have seen on TV," she said with a smile. "Since you've been through so much, let me give you a present as a welcoming gift." With that, she pulled out a large, somewhat ornate digital watch. "This watch has many functions that you may find interesting, and as long as you are here, please wear it. There is a little book on the night table in your room that gives all the directions, but its most important function is as a pager. When this vibrates, dial the number shown on any phone around here, and you will be connected immediately."

Tom removed his own watch and started to place it in his pocket. "Sir, I will put it in storage for you, and you can pick it up when you leave," said the Lt., indicating a row of lockboxes. "Also, I think you will find this useful, handing Tom a black-leather bound object. Inside the leather sheath, Tom found a black scout-like pocketknife. "It seems that many of the soda cans don't open just right, so you will find the opener function to be very useful." said the Lieutenant. "Thank you," said Tom, "but I have my own knife right here," as he reached into his pocket. Then he tried his other pocket; then he checked his other pockets. "Darn it, I seem to have misplaced it. But I'll borrow yours until I can find mine."

"Meanwhile, don't worry about it," said Dr. Ruth. "I'm sure you will want to get freshened up, so I will show you to your room."

"I'd rather have answers," said Tom. "All in good time," said Ruth, turning toward another door and starting to walk away from the desk. "Sir, just a minute, you'll need this," the Lieutenant said, handing Tom a light gray plastic card. "This is your key and ID card. It will open any door you are authorized to enter." Tom took it and noticed it had a picture of him on it wearing the same clothes he had on now. "Where did they get my picture?" He thought, trying to sneak a peek around the room looking for a camera.

Before he could spot the camera, Ruth led him through the door and down a short hallway to an ordinary elevator. "Your room is on level 3, room 12a," she said as the elevator door opened. They stepped in, and she punched 3 on the control panel. Tom noted that there appeared to be at least 20 floors. "Please remember to keep your card with you at all times because without it, no door will open, including this elevator." By then, the elevator had arrived at its destination, and the door opened into a hallway resembling a very high-quality and expensive hotel floor. "Your room is down here," said Ruth, walking quickly through the plush carpeting. At number 12a, she pointed to a card slot beside the door. "Put your card in there and open the door." Tom did so and, upon stepping into the room, received another surprise.

The room was a suite of rooms, all very tastefully furnished, with all the amenities offered by at least a 4-star hotel. Ruth breezed through the room, pointing out some of the goodies, including the huge HDTV, jacuzzi tub, and steam shower. In the bedroom, she showed him a closet with clothing and shoes. "Since you didn't have time to pack, I requested our commissary to send up something. I think that these will fit you, and you should find underwear in the bureau over there. If you would like a snack, we have 24-hour room service. Just dial 'rs' on the phone over there. Oh, yes, to save you the trouble, there are no outside lines. This phone is just for use in the complex. But please feel free to try. While you are waiting, you may want to clean up. Dr. Kafka is not available right now. He's outside and isn't expected to be back until later. But he will answer all your questions when you see him. Anything else? No, then I'll probably see you later."

With that, Ruth turned and walked out quietly, shutting the door behind her. Tom stammered a minute, trying to get his thoughts caught up with what was happening, and said, "Wait." When he tried the door she had just gone through, it was locked, and no amount of pulling or turning worked, nor would his card open the door. "I guess I just need a bath before they let me out into the local population," he thought as he finally resigned himself to not getting out until someone let him out.

After his bath, he explored the room and its amenities. The small refrigerator was well stocked with the usual assortment of snacks and his favorite beer. The entertainment center housed a huge HDTV plus a DVD/CD player. It also housed an assortment of liquors that were in the stratospheric price range. He knew this because he had found the receipt from the grocery store for Mary's purchase of a small gift bottle for his last birthday. And here were full-liter bottles. "Well, since I'm stuck, I might as well learn to live with it," he thought as he poured himself a healthy shot of a single malt scotch he had only read about and had never been able to find in the places he could afford to shop on his teacher's salary. It was every bit as good as the write-up had said, if not better.

"He looks like he has adjusted to his quarters," said Dr. Ruth, MD, PhD, PhD. Her two PhD's were in psychiatry and pharmacology. "He's actually doing better than some of the others," she observed as she turned to her colleague sitting next to her, watching the large flat plasma screen display of Tom's suite. "Let's let him finish his drink before we put him to bed and start turning the key," said the tall, heavyset

Man seated next to her. "Tomorrow, we'll continue the treatment, and by Thursday or Friday at the latest, he'll be ready to join the team," said Dr. R. Kafka, the director of Project Pyramid.

Tom continued to enjoy the scotch, oblivious to those discussions. Gradually, he began to relax, and when the two attendants entered, he was fully asleep. He didn't even move when they carried him to the king-size bed and gently covered him.

The next morning, or so it said on his bedside clock, Tom felt very refreshed and quite hungry. He thought he was home and that it had all been a dream. But when he propped one eye open and looked around the room, it wasn't a dream. "This can't be real. This stuff only happens to spies and secret agents, not elementary school teachers," he thought. Yet he had to face the fact that this was not his room, and he had on the watch that woman, Dr. Ruth, gave him. Plus, these were not his clothes, so he had to accept the inevitable and dial the RS number to order breakfast. Room service was very fast. He had had very little time to shower and dress before there was a knock at the door. When he said, "Come in," Dr. Ruth walked in, pushing a service cart loaded with food. She was wearing a bright pink pantsuit with a white silk-like fluffy blouse and a big bright smile. "I thought you might like some company while you eat, and we can talk about why you are here. If it's OK with you, Dr. Kafka would like to join us for coffee."

During breakfast, Dr. Ruth played the part of the perfect hostess, serving the eggs benedict and perfectly broiled grapefruit topped with maraschino cherry juice. After the main course, she topped the whole meal with banana flambé served over the most wonderful vanilla ice cream Tom had ever tasted. When Tom complimented the meal, Dr. Ruth positively beamed, "Smith is on loan to us from the Navy. He used to be a personal chef to one of the joint chiefs of staff but got a little too carried away with his choice of wines and liquors, and the ensuing bill would take him two lifetimes to pay off at regular navy pay. Of course, working for us, he will repay his bill in a relatively short time, and then, I suspect, we will have to give him up. But for now, he's all ours."

"Well, I've rested, eaten, and still cannot contact my wife. What's going to happen next?" said Tom.

"I believe that I can answer that question," said the large, heavyset man standing in the open doorway.

"I didn't hear you come in," said Tom.

"It's a wonder you even heard me at all since you were caught in Ruth's captivating web. She can be very consuming of all your senses, you know," said the Man. "But enough of the small talk. My name is Dr. Kafka, and I am the director of Project Pyramid."

"Ok, Doc. Why am I here? Why am I being kept in isolation? When will I be allowed to go home? And why me?" asked Tom in a flurry of questions.

"Ok, take it easy," laughed Dr. Kafka. "You are right in asking your questions, and I shall answer them to the best of my ability. But before I do, let me give you a little history lesson, you know, like you give your students. And since your minor was history, I should think you would find this very interesting."

"I'm all yours," muttered Tom.

"First, let me sit down and share some of that delicious coffee Smith made for you."

"Please do," said Dr. Ruth, reaching for another cup and saucer from under the food service cart.

"To begin, what do you know about the Vietnam War, Tom?"

"Not much. I spent most of my free time trying to make good grades and stay out of the draft," said Tom.

"Well, Tom, over the next few days, I suspect you will find that you know a bit more than you can remember now, but more on that later," said Dr. Kafka. "The Vietnam War was a very troubling time for our country; we were fighting on many fronts. Civil rights, confusion about why our boys were there, and the ensuing cold war. Technology was the buzzword, and it was cutting into everything we knew about our world, ourselves, and our relationships with others. Aids was starting to be identified. We found that the more we depended on technology, the more vulnerable we were. Why, at one time, a nuclear bomb exploded over a certain area of our country."

"Longitude 0000, Latitude 0000," muttered Tom, who then looked up to find both doctors staring at him intently and immediately felt his face getting very flushed.

"Do you know what you just said?" asked Dr. K.

"I don't know. Must have read it somewhere," said Tom.

"That information has never been released," said Dr. K.

"Then I guess it was just a lucky guess," said Tom, "but go ahead with the history lesson so you can answer my questions or at least let me go."

Dr. K glanced at Dr. R and continued, "During that time, it was discovered that both the Russians and the U.S. could completely destroy each other many times over and were pledged to do so if attacked. It was called MAD, Mutually Assured Destruction, and let me say it was a lousy way to win a war by destroying the world. At that time, several scenarios were conducted by a secret think tank located just outside of Ivor, Virginia."

"Yeah, the Martian Exchange," interrupted Tom. "But that's old history. What about now?"

This time, Dr. Ruth popped a meaningful glance at Dr. Kafka.

"To continue, several scenarios were developed. First, if civilization as we know it were to be destroyed, what would the survivors need to know to survive? Second, what if all our electronic storage was destroyed? How soon can we rebuild meaningful data? Finally, could we develop an easily transportable storage system capable of storing incredible amounts of information, not dependent on outside power sources and relatively immune to data degrading normally found in storage media at that time? That was a tall set of specs for any project. The priority to solving this was both urgent and secret. The Russians knew we were up to something and spent much time and money trying to find out about us. In fact, if they only knew, they helped fund part of the project by paying bribes to people they thought might have some knowledge of the project. Such is the irony of the Cold War," chuckled Dr. Kafka. "I was a special scientific advisor to President Kennedy for agriculture. In reality, I was one of the three project directors working on this problem, hence the name Project Pyramid, with each of us being responsible for a different corner of the pyramid. Thompson was to decide what data was important and how to condense or encode it. Shapiro oversaw designing the storage system, and I was assigned to quality control and monitoring of the process. We finally developed the ideal storage system of the time, one that didn't depend on outdated technology, difficult to locate energy sources, one that was self-renewing and easily transportable. Congratulations, Mr. Roberts, you were the result of several billions of black ops money, countless man and woman hours of work, and the sacrifices of a number of people, including a president of the United States."

Tom stopped drinking coffee, dropped the cup, and started coughing violently. "Dr. Kafka, you've got to be kidding," he said between coughs. "I think you have been sampling too many drugs from that time. I'm just an elementary school teacher, married, with children, and a hell of a mortgage. And I've got the memories to prove it. Just ask me. I remember my life quite well," challenged Tom.

"That's the beauty of the program," continued Dr. Kafka. "The subject was loaded with information and given a deep conditioning and false background better than that found in any witness protection program. Over the course of the years, we have been monitoring our storage units or subjects to see how well the walls that we built were holding up and the quality of data storage.

"No way!" said Tom, practically shouting. "I know who I am. I would know if someone's been messing with my mind."

"Are you sure?" said Dr. Kafka. "And please sit down. You'll need to be if you want to hear the rest of the story."

"Ok, then," said Tom, sitting down. "If what you say was true, then who was I, or am I, or whatever?" said Tom.

Why me?

Dr. Ruth looked at Dr. Kafka. "Go ahead and tell him," said Dr. Kafka. Ruth reached under the serving cart and extracted a bright orange file. "Your name was Tom Edison. You were named after a distant relative, Thomas Edison. You attended the University of Florida in Gainesville, Florida. You graduated with honors in psychology and entered the Air Force as a Second Lieutenant on July 12, 1969. You served in Vietnam on General Westmoreland's staff as intelligence liaison. You rapidly rose to the rank of Major and earned several decorations for outstanding service to your country." Dr. R held up a photograph of a smiling young man in Air Force fatigues wearing Major's oak leaves who looked kind of like a younger Tom. What brought you to our attention was the receipt of a letter from you suggesting a very similar need to develop contingency plans and protocols that were too close for comfort to what we were trying to accomplish."

"Due to the nature of the project and its importance, we were faced with a dilemma," interjected Dr. Kafka. "You had guessed too much and couldn't be allowed to express your ideas any further than you had already done. So, we basically had two choices: eliminate you by either putting you in a federal prison or special hospital for the rest of your life, use extreme prejudice, or bring you on board."

"In your case, the decision was made to bring you on board. You were bright, eager, and enthusiastic. In fact, you helped develop some of the encoding protocols for the program. And in the end, you were one of our most viable subjects. You were programmed near the end of the project with some of the most extensive and complicated data we had to store. You were and still are one of the best subjects we ever had in the program," said Dr. Ruth, looking up from the folder and giving Tom a hundred-dollar smile.

Tom sat still for several minutes with his hands folded in front of him. Finally, he said, "You're full of crap! I don't know what you are trying to do or why, but let me go now."

"Tom, let's be logical. Why would we go to all this trouble and expense to bring you, a nobody by your admission, to a top-secret government installation, wine, and dine you, just for your pleasant personality? Not to mention antagonizing several rather influential members of Congress? Think about it. Why would your government do such a thing?" said Dr. Kafka. "You are a VIP, and we will help you to learn about it over the next few days. Then you decide what you think about the project, but just give us a few days. We'll also reimburse you very well for your consulting."

"What about Mary? I want to be able to talk to her now," demanded Tom.

"That will happen shortly," said Dr. Ruth, "but you will need to have one of our security people with you to help you avoid any breaches of security, which I'm sure you can understand if half of what we say is true," said Dr. Kafka.

"How much are we talking about, and for how long?" said Tom. "Also, I want a copy of a written contract given to my wife."

"No problem," said Dr. Kafka, and the amount will be our standard contract amount of, say, $1500 per day plus any expenses, of course," said Dr. Kafka, sticking his hand out. "Deal?"

"Deal," said Tom, reaching across the table and shaking Dr. Kafka's hand. "How soon will you have the contract," said Tom.

"I just happen to have our standard consultant's contract here," said Dr. Ruth, pulling a multipage legal-size stack of papers from the orange folder. "This contract also includes the Secrets Act Amendment, which basically says that if you talk about this project outside of those with proper clearance and need to know, you go to jail. Any other questions?" she asked, passing him the packet and handing Tom a silver pen. "Please read and initial each page where indicated. If you have any questions, please ask them. We'll wait here, so take your time and let us know when you are finished. We will give your wife a copy of the contract later today after you call her."

When Tom finished signing at least two reams of paper, or so it seemed, he handed the stack to Dr. Ruth and said, "Well, that's done. What's next, or when do we start?"

"Shortly," said Dr. R. "As soon as we process the paperwork to bring you aboard, then you'll get your phone call and get going." With that statement, she stood up with Dr. Kafka and left.

In the hall outside the suite, Dr. Kafka turned to her and said, "May I have it back?"

"Of course," said Dr. R as she handed him the vile containing a small pink pill that would have induced a heart attack when placed in someone's food or coffee and which would have been given to Tom if he had not agreed to participate in the project.

Chapter 5

After his visit with Tom, Dr. Kafka caught the elevator down to level 12, the combat level. This level was used to conduct various training scenarios to keep the security detachment on their toes and ready to handle any foreseeable problems that might arise in the complex. His director of security consistently "tweaked" the various offerings on level 12, until it was whispered among the troops that only God could survive more than five minutes there.

In a few minutes, Dr. Kafka would select a bodyguard for Tom from two candidates who were to be tested today. Both had excellent pedigrees, were skilled in at least two or three forms of martial arts, rated as experts with every weapon used in NATO, and were excellent swimmers and SCUBA divers. Each was essentially the equivalent of Navy SEALs, Army Rangers, and Green Berets rolled into one. They both had advanced degrees—hers in physics, his in chemistry. He could speak at least two languages fluently, possibly more. By the end of today, only one would remain. The winner would be Tom's companion and security escort. The loser would be invited to join the NSA.

The elevator door opened into a small room with a big "Declare Your Weapons" sign facing passengers as they exited. Dr. Kafka knew he had exactly two minutes to declare any weapons he was carrying. Failure to do so would result in incapacitation and some very unpleasant interrogation by his security chief.

"I have a 9mm S&W," stated Dr. Kafka.

"You are cleared to enter, Dr. Kafka," responded a disembodied voice. "Candidate One is in Room A, and Candidate Two is in Room C, as you requested."

"Thank you," said Dr. Kafka as he entered a second room with five doors marked A through D and Control Room. He entered Room C, faced the young man, and said:

"Today's exercise will entail your capturing an enemy and placing that enemy in a container at the bus station for transportation out of here. When the bell rings, enter the door, find your opponent, overcome him or her. Do not kill them. Put that person in the box and exit through this door. Please wait until the bell rings."

Dr. Kafka then went to Room A and repeated the same instructions. From there, he went to the control booth, checked the interior monitors, and turned down the lights to simulate a moonless night on what appeared to be a small mall and residential street. Then he rang the bell.

"Let the games begin!" he thought.

****

When the bell rang, the differences in combat styles became immediately apparent. The young man kicked the door open, immediately charged out, cut left, then right, and stopped behind a dumpster against the far wall. The young woman cautiously opened her door, turned off the light in her room, and stayed well back in the shadows as she surveyed the surroundings. She slipped out, crossing the simulated street to a doorway. Testing the door, she found it locked.

Meanwhile, the man had surveyed most of the area around his exit. He found an open door, climbed up an interior ladder to the third floor, and scanned the surroundings. The woman began circling the perimeter of the combat area. The young man spotted her first but lost her when she moved behind a building corner about 200 feet away, heading to his left. He reasoned he could intercept her as she turned the corner toward his location. Descending the ladder, he backed into a doorway, carefully watching the building corner where she would appear.

As he eased most of his body into the doorway, he heard a faint rustle of cloth or scrape of a crepe-soled shoe, then saw stars. His excellent conditioning and quick reflexes saved him from being completely knocked out as he jumped away from the sound. He had caught a glancing blow to the head—enough to daze him—but managed a back kick before staggering away. The satisfying feel of his foot connecting with something soft was scant comfort against the ringing in his ears. He stumbled into another doorway, slowing his breathing and trying to shake off the headache building in his skull.

The woman had the breath knocked out of her and rolled to the side of the street, assuming her opponent would be on top of her. Her tingling hand told her that her opponent either had an extraordinarily thick skull or was wearing a helmet. Either way, she had no desire to fight him in her current condition. As her vision cleared from red back to the shadowy night, she realized he was not nearby.

"So much for the element of surprise," she thought. "Now I've got to work to finish this job, and I've only got 40 minutes left."

***

Why me?

The man reasoned that his opponent was almost as skilled as he was, though not quite. Circling back, he expected to find her incapacitated—his kick should have left her unconscious or at least severely weakened. But she was gone. The fact that she had survived his kick made him raise both his respect and his alertness.

Hearing a faint sound, he turned, hands raised to attack. He spotted the edge of a shoe dragging itself slowly around the corner of the building ahead. I did get her, he thought. Quickly, but cautiously, he approached the corner and peeked around. There, he saw a leg struggling to push into a doorway. In a swift stride, he covered the distance, grabbed the leg, and stomped where the person's stomach should have been—if there had been a person attached to the leg.

Stopping to look up, he met a rock-hard foot that snapped his head back. His last conscious thought was: What kind of person wears pantyhose on an assault job?

***

The woman retrieved her pantyhose and used one leg to tie the man's hands behind him and the other to secure his feet. Dragging his heavy, unconscious body to the bus station, she noticed him starting to stir. His incredible discipline allowed him to keep silent and merely open his eyes. Seeing this, she applied pressure to a couple of arteries, and he went back to sleep. She shoved him into the box, closed the lid, and returned to her exit door.

As she entered, a faint sound warned her to duck just as a sap whooshed over her head. Executing a foot sweep in the pitch darkness, she connected with a set of legs and heard a satisfying clunk as her attacker hit the wall. Moving toward the remembered location of the light switch, she flipped it on, scanned the room, and saw the unconscious form of her assailant.

The door by the switch opened. She spun into a ready stance, only to see Dr. Kafka.

"Congratulations, Ms. Anderson. You've got the job. Take the rest of the day off and report to my office at 0900 hours tomorrow." He turned and left her standing there.

The door reopened, and several men entered. She dropped into her fighting stance.

"Hold it, girl, it's over! You've won," said an older man. "We're the medical team here to tend to the two people you stopped. Go on out—you've set a new record for the fastest time. You're incredible."

"You may want to put these on," he added, tossing her a pair of loose surgical pants. It was then she remembered she had used her pants to stuff her pantyhose and was currently bare below the waist.

The younger medic eyed her with a grin. "You want me to check you over for any damage?" he asked, smiling.

"No thanks," she replied. "A nice shower will be all I need."

"If you change your mind or need help scrubbing your back, I'll be on duty at the infirmary. You know—911. Just give me a call," he added hopefully.

"Thanks, I'll remember that," she said, walking out into the hallway. The pain in her side from the kick and her hand from "Mr. Hardhead" made her doubt she would make it back to her room, but she'd be damned if she would call what's-his-name for help.

Later, after a long shower, May lay naked on her bed, too tired to even put on her usual modest pajamas. As she drifted off to sleep, she thought, what have I gotten myself into?

Chapter 6

The next morning, May's phone started chirping.

"What the hell?" she muttered, trying to hit the snooze button on the radio by the bed.

When she finally realized her error and lifted the receiver, a pleasant voice said, "Miss Anderson, Dr. Kafka would like you to join him for breakfast in the executive dining room instead of his office for your 9 o'clock meeting."

"OK," muttered May. "By the way, what time is it?"

"8:45," said the cheery voice on the other end and disconnected.

"8:45," she repeated. Suddenly, the significance of that number dawned on May. When she tried to jump out of bed, the actions of the night before became painfully apparent. But with a groan, she made it to her closet and tried to focus on what to wear. Fortunately, it was easy to dress since she didn't have to undress from her nightclothes. She threw on her dress—her only dress, since she usually wore pants— and beat her best time for putting on pantyhose and low-heeled pumps. Luckily, she had her summer short haircut and only needed to brush it a little while using her other hand to brush her teeth. She was out the door in seven minutes from the time the phone rang. She was glad she wasn't meeting someone wearing a swimsuit, as the big bruise from that kick last night would look worse before it got better.

"Now, if only the aspirin I took would kick in, I might be able to stand up straight when I meet the boss," she thought.

May entered the dining room and realized she had never been to the executive dining room before. She couldn't see a door labeled Executives from where she stood, so she had to ask one of the busboys where that elusive place was located.

"Why, it's one level up, through the door marked 1600. Well, so much for being on time," she thought, as she dashed up the stairs rather than taking the slow elevator. She burst out of the stairwell, nearly knocking over another woman who had just started to open the stairwell door.

"What the hell? Watch where you're going," May heard as she headed for a set of wooden doors with a big 1600 on them.

"Something about that number," thought May as she slowed down to enter the doors in a more sedate fashion.

Inside, she spotted Dr. Kafka seated in a corner booth. As she approached, he pointedly glanced at his watch and then at her but didn't say anything about her being two and a half minutes late.

"I'm glad you got my message, Miss Anderson, about the change in meeting places. Would you care for something to eat? The crêpes are very good," he said as he rose to meet her and shake her hand.

May tried not to wince at the pressure on her sore hand as she thanked him. "Yes, I would like some crêpes with strawberries. Thank you."

Dr. Kafka placed her order with a waiter who magically appeared at the side of the table. After the waiter left, Dr. Kafka turned to May and asked, "How are you doing? You took a pretty good kick last night."

"I'm fine," she said, trying to keep from groaning out the words.

Dr. Kafka looked at her for a second, as if he really did believe her, but didn't tell her that he knew exactly how she was feeling. He didn't feel it was important to mention that after her bath, when she lay down on her bed, the medics had introduced a mild sleeping gas into her room. The older medic, a very respected neurosurgeon, and the younger one, a noted internist, had checked her while she slept. They had X-rayed her, tested her for any internal damage, repositioned her, and left. They then flushed out the gas and let her sleep until his secretary called that morning.

Dr. Kafka thought the fact that she was walking and talking at all attested to a very strong constitution and a determined personality. The other two people involved in last night's test were still in the base infirmary—one with a mild to moderate concussion and the other with a dislocated knee and a broken nose.

"While we are waiting, let's get on to business," said Dr. Kafka. "First, again, let me congratulate you on a splendid job. You set some sort of record that has our chief of security foaming, since it was his record you broke. But enough of that. More coffee?"

By then, the waiter appeared with a silver coffee pot, poured the coffee, and left without saying a word.

"Due to your success last night and your background, I'm prepared to offer you a contract for one year. The pay is G-5, plus expenses. What do you say?"

May looked at Dr. Kafka, smiled, and said, "I'd love to. However, you appear to have overlooked telling me what my specific services are to be. I am not a bimbo and do not want to be a spy or secret agent. If this job is one of those, then you've got the wrong person."

"No, it's not that. You are to be assigned as an assistant to a very remarkable gentleman and protect him to the best of your considerable ability. You'll probably spend most of your time just keeping him from getting lost inside this complex. When he goes outside the complex, you will accompany him as his secretary. But your main job will be to act as a bodyguard, that's all. When we finish, the remainder of your contract will be paid off, and you will be given a choice of other assignments within our organization, or you may resign. What do you say?"

May thought about it for a moment. "Why not? I've nothing better in my life, and this could be a nice rest after the last two years of trying to become Miss He-Woman." Then she said aloud, "Only if I don't have to sleep with him. I am not for hire as a whore."

"Deal," said Dr. Kafka, offering his hand.

After May had shaken Dr. Kafka's hand, the food suddenly appeared. The crêpes were done to perfection and stuffed with a delicious cheese. The side dishes included fresh strawberries, sour cream, and blueberries. Another dish held a thick slice of Virginia hickory-smoked ham with a delicious aroma that proclaimed its heritage to all at the table.

"By the way, you know that since we are a government agency, all our work falls under the Secrets Act. If you'll just read this contract while you're eating and sign where indicated. If you have any questions, please ask them," Dr. Kafka said, producing the equivalent of a bound workbook.

May almost choked when he produced the document, "Well, it is government work, and you know how long-winded the government can be. Most of this covers the terms and benefits to your heirs, if you have any. Do you?"

May shook her head, "Plus, there is a copy of the Secrets Act, which basically says if you talk about anything you see here without written clearance from me or someone higher up, then this contract is null and void, and you go to jail, that's all. Would you pass the cream, please?" said Dr. Kafka.

May finally got through the contract, signed where indicated, and handed it to Dr. Kafka.

"You can pick up a copy in my office this afternoon," said Dr. Kafka. Glancing at his watch, he added, "We need to get you processed into our family here, so please report to Level 18, Room 9. You will need this card to get there. You must arrive by 1300 hours since this card expires at that time. If you are not in Room 9 by then, I'm afraid some very unpleasant people will come looking for you and will ask some very unpleasant questions."

With that, Dr. Kafka stood, excused himself, and left, leaving May pondering what she had just done and subvocally asking herself, "Why me?"

May pondered her question as she finished her breakfast. She reviewed her short life: earning her degrees, the physical challenges of learning the various disciplines of hand-to-hand combat, and the special program where the government was studying the effectiveness of teaching women to use "real" firearms like the Navy SEALs and Army Rangers used in covert operations. Then there were the real reasons for doing what she did: the failed affair with the acting chair of the physics department at the university.

He had kept leading her on, saying he wanted to marry her when she got her Ph.D. so they could both get teaching/research assignments together. When she was nearing the completion of her master's degree, she found out that the "additional research" he had been doing at the lab had not involved pure physics but physiology research—with one grad assistant from history. Apparently, they were reviewing the historical development of the Kama Sutra and attempting to duplicate all the positions of lovemaking listed therein.

May had then taken out her anger on any other male in her hand-to-hand combat classes. Many men had learned the hard way not to get involved with her, whether with a trip to the local drugstore for a gallon of liniment at best, or to the local emergency room for stitches or a cast at worst. Gradually, she had worked off her anger at men in general—and at onc man in particular—to the point that when he made an inappropriate comment to her at a local lounge while fondling another person, she had merely knocked out a couple of his teeth. One of those teeth she had kept for several months before throwing it away in the pigsty at the university.

"More coffee, miss?" a voice interrupted, waking her out of her self-evaluation.

"I'm sorry, what did you say?" she replied.

"Would you care for more coffee or something else?" replied the waiter, a Ph.D. in psychology whose job was to observe the executive diners for possible stress symptoms and report them to Dr. Kafka.

May looked at the young man, gave a faint smile, and said, "No thanks. I've got to get to Room 9 for my medical, and I want to have something in my pee besides caffeine."

"I understand," said the waiter, unsuccessfully trying to keep from chuckling.

"By the way, what time is it?" asked May.

"Nearly one o'clock," said the waiter.

"Where is Room 9?" asked May.

"You probably passed it on the way down to the lower levels. It's right on the first floor, just around the corner from the elevator. You can't miss it," said the young waiter.

"Thanks," said May, trying to get up gracefully, yet still being reminded in a very sore, direct way, about yesterday's action.

The net result was a slight "ouch" and a touch of sweat on her upper lip, all of which was duly noted by the waiter, who continued to observe her in a slightly unprofessional manner as May walked from the room.

May uttered an "OS" (oh shit) as she stepped from the elevator. The wall clock said 12:58, and she didn't have the slightest idea which way to go since she couldn't see any room numbers from the elevator. Luckily, an older lady came around the corner just then.

"Which way to Room 9?"

"Why, that way," said the lady, pointing to the left.

May took off at a run, just slipping her card into the required slot as the clock clicked to 1:00. She held her breath as there seemed to be a pause before the slot decided to accept the card. Finally, the card disappeared, and the door clicked open.

Inside, the infirmary looked just like any other small but well-equipped emergency room May had seen. The older medic from last night was reading some sort of medical magazine and looked up as she entered.

"Hi," he said. "You must be here for your pre-employment medical. Dr. Kafka's office said they were sending you down."

"What do I have to do to get through with this?" asked May.

"Well, let's get some blood, urine, and some X-rays. Then, I'll check to see if your heart is still ticking. That's about it."

"OK, let's get going. I'm in a hurry," said May, who didn't want to admit how much she hated needles and wanted to get this over with as soon as possible.

The medic moved with professionalism and consideration, both of which were noted by May.

"You know, for a medic, you sure seem to know your stuff," she commented.

"Thank you," said the medic, neglecting to mention that they had already run these tests last night while she was asleep from the gas.

"When will you have the results so I'll know if I got a job or have to go?"

"Well, don't you have to pick up some papers in Dr. Kafka's office?"

"Yes," replied May.

"Good. Why don't you do that now, and I can call in the results to the secretary. OK?"

"OK," said May. "But how do I get down there when my card has expired?"

"Here's one that will get you down there, but don't go anywhere else."

"Later," said May as she walked toward the door, trying not to show how sore she was from last night.

"Oh, just a minute," said the medic. "I notice you're a bit stiff from your test last night. You might want to stop by the ladies' room and rub some of this on your sore spots. The restroom is on your way to Dr. Kafka's office," he said, tossing her a tube of some ointment. "It will give me a little extra time to finish your tests. And your card will work the restroom door."

"OK," said May.

On the way, May did stop by the ladies' room and rubbed some of the ointment on. Glory be, the aching stopped within seconds!

"I've got to get more of this stuff," said May, not knowing that the tube was the result of several million dollars of taxpayers' money and currently only available to Special Ops field personnel.

The liniment worked so well that by the time May got to Dr. Kafka's office, she could stand up and walk without limping or groaning. At the door, she looked for a slot for the card and, not seeing one, tried the door. It opened to a very simple waiting room, done in early government style, with the usual vinyl-covered couch, green institutional carpeting, and a grotesque Formica coffee table.

"This certainly isn't the homey western-country motif I recall from my first interview," thought May. As she looked around the room, she noticed a card slot set in the coffee table.

"I guess I'm supposed to put my card in there," she thought.

When she inserted her card, she heard a click, and a door to her left opened. Inside, she could see the older woman seated at a high-top circular receptionist desk who had given her directions to the elevator.

"Come on in," said the woman, smiling at May.

"I must be in the wrong office," said May. "This isn't the office I'm supposed to meet Dr. Kafka in, is it?"

"It certainly is," said the woman. "This is the employee reception room. The other room is for visitors. Just a sec," she said, typing something on a keyboard that appeared to have more keys than a standard one.

May recalled seeing something similar in the advanced thermonuclear lab at the university during a brief tour for one of her classes. But this one looked far more complicated than the one she remembered. As May got closer, she saw the high-top desk housed several very high-resolution monitors, at least 21 inches or bigger.

The woman finished typing and looked up. "We haven't met formally, but I know a lot about you. My name is Martha, although I'm called by other titles depending on who's mad at Dr. Kafka," she said as she stood to shake hands with May.

"Dr. Kafka is expecting you, so go right on in through that center door over there."

May started to ask Martha if she had ever been in the military because of her bearing. She would have been right. Martha had been one of the few female B-52 pilots in the Air Force, graduated at the top of her class at the Air Force Academy, and held a degree in mechanical engineering. Now, she was a senior administrative assistant to Dr. Kafka, with more responsibility than a B-52 pilot carrying nuclear bombs.

As the door clicked open, May thought it felt a bit too solid for an office door but didn't dwell on it. She was right, of course. The entire Command Center was reinforced concrete and lead-lined. The doors were a special titanium-and-steel combination that would require much more than most people would suspect to breach them.

Inside was Dr. Kafka's office as she remembered it, with him seated behind his desk. When she came in, he rose and warmly greeted her with a handshake as he guided her to a group of chairs arranged by the fireplace.

"Congratulations," said Dr. Kafka. "You passed everything, your physical was great, and you have demonstrated that you can do the job. Here is a copy of your contract. And, as of ten minutes ago, you are collecting government pay."

"Thank you," said May, accepting the rather heavy document. "But just what is my assignment?"

"You are to be a personal assistant and bodyguard to a gentleman who, I suspect, doesn't realize just how important he is. As far as he is concerned, you are from the office pool, assigned to help him. You will have time where your 'other duties' will require you to be elsewhere, essentially in training to help you do your primary job of protecting him."

"That should be fairly simple," said May.

"You may think you know everything, and with your unique training, you do know a lot." At that moment, there was a discreet chime, "Come in, Martha," said Dr. Kafka.

Martha entered and handed Dr. Kafka a manila envelope, "Thank you. That will be all," said Dr. Kafka. Martha smiled at May, turned, and left.

"As I was saying, you do know a lot. But many things are not what they seem, and you will need to learn how to spot that. Let's continue this conversation during lunch. Why don't I meet you at 12:30? OK?"

May looked at her wrist to check the time but realized her watch was missing.

When she looked up, Dr. Kafka asked, "Is there a problem with that time?"

May said, "I seem to have misplaced my watch. What time do you have?"

"Let me see," said Dr. Kafka, opening the manila envelope and reading the time on a watch he pulled out. "Looks about 15 minutes from now. Is that right?" he said, handing her the watch.

When May looked at the watch, she jumped up and said, "This is my watch. How did you get it?"

"Like I said, things are not what they always seem. Martha removed it from your wrist when she shook hands, and she also planted a transmitter on you. See that little spot on the underside of your sleeve? That's a short-range audio transmitter. Everything we said for the last five minutes has been recorded. Martha, please bring in the recording."

Dr. Kafka's door opened, and Martha walked in with a small cassette recorder. Dr. Kafka pressed the play button, and May heard Dr. Kafka say, "Congratulations, you passed your physical..."

"Enough already. You made your point. Thank you for the lesson, Martha."

"You are welcome," said Martha, beaming a big smile.

Dr. Kafka turned to May and handed her the manila envelope, "Inside, you will find your ID, appointment times for your classes, and a schedule of times you will officially work with Tom. Unofficially, you are on 24/7 with him until the project is finished. Welcome aboard, and good luck. Now, let's go meet your charge."

Chapter 7

On the way down to Level 8, May began to have the little doubts that often arise when starting a new job. *Am I good enough? Do I really want to do this? Why me?* Almost as if he were reading her mind, Dr. Kafka turned and said, "Don't be too hard on yourself. Martha is among the best at what she does, and this is a good way to reinforce the concept that one must always stay on their toes in this job. Otherwise, somebody might get killed or hurt."

May made a mental note to herself. *Not on my shift,* she thought. They turned a corner and came to another checkpoint, where a young officer sat at the standard-issue obnoxious gray government desk and chair. Dr. Kafka showed his ID to the officer, who scrutinized it very carefully. Then he stepped through the door behind the desk.

May followed suit, showing her card, which—after seemingly long scrutiny—allowed her to pass through the door as well. Once through, she found herself and Dr. Kafka in a small secondary office with two unmarked doors on opposite walls, each with a card slot beside it. Dr. Kafka pointed to the door on the right.

Why me?

"If you go through that door, there's a good possibility you may not come out. Always go through the door on the left," he said, inserting his card into the slot by the left-hand door. There was a click, and the door opened to reveal what appeared to be another clinic of some kind. Several men and women in lab coats of various colors were all staring at a man resting on a couch, wearing a bizarre-looking helmet with numerous wires connected to several racks of equipment.

"Guess who's your charge," said Dr. Kafka.

"The one with the funny hat," May replied.

"Right. I think they're just about finished with this run," said Dr. Kafka, leading the way over to the couch, where the technicians were lifting the helmet off the man's head.

As Tom looked up, he appeared slightly dazed and disoriented. As Dr. Kafka approached, Tom began to connect with his surroundings.

"Hi, Dr. Kafka," said Tom.

"Well, Tom, how do you feel now?"

"Feels like I've been on one hell of a trip. If you ever put that thing on the market, you'll probably put most drug dealers out of business."

"Is all this starting to make sense now?" asked Dr. Kafka.

"Some of it," said Tom, "but I'm still confused about a lot of the facts. I know you're kind of looking into my memories layer by layer, and as you open them up, I'm starting to remember some things from before. But there's still a lot of confusion, and I'm still having trouble remembering."

"Don't worry about it. Most of our memory banks have the same problems until they're opened up and have had time to digest what happened in their other lives," lied Dr. Kafka.

In reality, 38% of the others had gone completely mad and were now housed in a very special sanitarium near the Ivor, Virginia, facility. With 50% of the other test subjects, the data had been corrupted through either the use of drugs or exposure to severe psychological trauma. Only 12% had progressed this far in downloading untainted information.

"Well, Tom, allow me to introduce you to your new part-time assistant. She'll serve as a kind of extra memory for you while you're adjusting to the process. May, meet Mr. Tom Roberts. Ms. Anderson, Mr. Roberts."

"I appreciate the offer, Dr. Kafka, but I really don't see the need for an assistant. I'm just a kind of walking book. People open me up and then put me back on the shelf. So, why do I need an assistant?"

"For one thing, she can help you get to your appointments on time. I can't have you wandering around lost in this complex like the last two times. Plus, you need to start documenting what you're remembering. May will help with that process. And since her duties are split between several departments, she won't be around all the time. But I think you'll find her to be a valuable asset to the team. You might want to take a walk and get acquainted. Meet Ruth for lunch and bring her up to date on how things are going."

"Who's Ruth?" asked Tom.

"The receptionist you met the first night. I find people are more comfortable talking to her than to me. Now, go on. I need to speak with the lab team."

May helped Tom up from the couch, catching him just as he stumbled.

"Sorry," he muttered. "Those treatments leave me a bit disoriented for a while."

"Maybe a little walk outside will help clear your mind," said May, still holding his arm in a firm grip.

"I think I can handle that, if you know where outside is," Tom replied.

Chapter 8

Outside the entrance to the ranch, they walked along and talked. The day promised to be very hot, so they each took a water bottle conveniently located in the cooler on the front porch. Tom asked Henry, the old Mexican sitting on the porch, what the best way to walk was.

"It depends on what you want to do. If you want to exercise, go toward the cell tower," he said with a wink at Tom. "There's a secluded area about a mile that way. No worries. It's still on the property. Just remember, whichever way you leave, come back the same way. Wouldn't want you mistaken for someone who shouldn't be here," said Henry.

"You mean your other entrances?" asked Tom.

"Sure," replied Henry. "How do you think we bring stuff in? Coming in from several different entrances makes it hard for somebody to figure out who's really here."

"I think we'll just head south," muttered Tom.

"Fine with me. Just don't wake me when you come back. It's time for my nap," said Henry.

As they walked along, Tom and May talked about their lives and the different things they had learned about their pasts.

"You know, prior to coming here, my life would have been simple. I plan to retire at the end of this year and then spend time with Mary and possibly the kids just fishing, and maybe doing a little writing. But now that has changed. Now I'm spending my time with a very fine young lady, and instead of writing fiction, it turns out that I am living a story that is stranger than the fiction I wanted to write," said Tom.

"In a way, I'm in the same boat," said May. "I thought I had it all planned out. Get my PhD, move on in the academic world, make babies, and discover some interesting little facts to add to our knowledge base about physics. But then things happened—on September 11 last year. After that, I had other thoughts about what I wanted to do. Now I'm not sure if academics is what I really want," said May.

"Well, look at it this way. In every cloud, there's some good. If the terrorists hadn't been forced to attack the Pentagon instead of the White House, those hidden rooms with their forgotten codes wouldn't have been discovered, and we wouldn't be having this conversation," said Tom.

They continued the rest of the walk, talking comfortably with each other.

When Tom and May arrived at the hacienda, Henry appeared to be sleeping on the front porch. In reality, he was keeping an eye on them through the little TV they thought was for regular programming. Instead, it was connected to a security feed from level 18. While Henry "slept," they quietly walked past him and met Dr. Ruth inside the front door at her desk.

"Well, did you have a nice walk?" she asked as they came in.

"This country is great if you like walking on Mars. Isn't there some green around here?" asked Tom.

"Oh, we tend to keep it cleared away for fire regulations. If a fire gets going out here, it can move faster than a horse can run, and DK would rather not have our staff out trying to fight it," said Dr. Ruth. Glancing at her watch, she looked up, gave them a winning smile, and said, "Looks like it's time for lunch."

After lunch, May attended to her other duties in another department, while Tom went back to the couch for more "unpeelings," as he called them. They settled into a regular schedule over the next few days: a morning meeting to review the day's needs, Tom returning to the couch, and May working with her department. They met again in the late afternoon for a short walk and dinner with the other project staff members. Afterward, Tom would review the day's results and tumble into bed, exhausted, only to be awakened the next morning by someone's idea of a humorous wake-up call.

One time, it was Louis Armstrong's version of reveille. Another time, a scramble klaxon had him awake and heading for the door before he knew what was happening. While he grumbled, he secretly looked forward to seeing what new ways they'd come up with to wake him.

The wake-up call was followed by a morning calisthenics class with other staff members. It seemed the only way to get breakfast was to earn a slip from one of the class leaders—a very attractive, full-figured young woman or a lean man who looked like he didn't just have a six-pack but the whole case. These attractive exteriors, however, housed the most ornery, dedicated workout fanatics whose sole interest seemed to be creating cardiac arrest in the motley crew assembled for morning torture. Yet, Tom noticed he started feeling better, lasting longer each day, and even losing weight—ten pounds in five days was nothing to sneeze at.

He was allowed to call Mary, acting as though he were at a conference, and assured her he'd be home by the end of the week. He checked in with a substitute who had his class under control and had no questions other than where the extra reading and math workbooks were stored. With that taken care of, Tom could focus on the increasingly interesting sessions.

Through these, he discovered more about his other life—a byproduct of the sessions. Soon, he found himself in the curious position of having two lives to choose from: the young Air Force Major or the elementary school teacher. "I wonder what Mary would say if she knew who the real me was," he thought.

Tom found Ruth, the receptionist, easy to talk to. She helped him start to make sense of his dual identity.

"You should be a counselor," he joked one evening.

"You're just being kind. All I'm doing is repeating what you say, like a living tape recorder. Besides, that would take a lot of academics, and I haven't been a student for a long time," Ruth said. This was true, as she had earned her MD at 25 and her first PhD at 27—over 20 years ago.

Tom laughed. "I know an elementary class that'll need a teacher soon. I think you'd be great."

"Thank you for the compliment," said Ruth, "but I think I'll stick with what I'm doing for a little while longer before considering any career changes."

Why me?

Chapter 9

Seven days after Tom first arrived, Dr. Kafka called both Tom and May in and brought them up to date on the results from the sessions.

"Tom, as you know, when the U.S. was attacked by terrorists on September 11, they also hit the Pentagon. What wasn't told to the public was that when the damage was being repaired, a very small room was discovered that had apparently been forgotten. It appeared on no blueprints and was found only when the builder had to tear out a partition to access some electrical wiring. In that room was a very old-fashioned safe. Inside the safe was this file. In this file were the destruct codes for three military facilities.

"Two of these facilities have been identified and verified, thanks to you. We are now trying to find the location of the third and most important one. We think that's why you are here. Over the last week, we have downloaded much of the information you have held in trust in your brain, but we must go deeper. So, starting tomorrow, we will add an extra session each day until we get that information," said Dr. Kafka.

"Because there is a slight risk to you by increasing the number of sessions, I am authorized to increase your fee by $500 per day as long as we have the extra sessions."

"What do you mean by 'slight risk'?" asked Tom.

"Nothing to worry about. There may be a temporary loss of memory of things that occurred before you were programmed."

"How long is temporary?" said Tom.

"We are not exactly sure. It could be a few minutes, a few days, or a few years."

"A few years?" exclaimed Tom, jumping to his feet. "My life as I know it could disappear just like that!" he said, snapping his fingers.

"Now relax," said Dr. Kafka. "We will monitor you every step of the way and will stop if we spot anything that may appear detrimental to you. Remember, if it affects you, it may also affect the project. So, we have a very strong interest in protecting you," said Dr. Kafka.

"I need a little time to consider this," said Tom.

"Take the rest of the day and let me know tomorrow morning," said Dr. Kafka.

Why me?

As they were leaving, Dr. Kafka turned to May and said, "May, would you mind giving me a few minutes to review some information from your other department?"

After Tom left, Dr. Kafka turned to May and said, "It has come to our attention that certain terrorist groups found out about the material uncovered during the attack. They apparently passed it on, or more likely sold it, to another terrorist organization whose leader the U.S. is currently seeking. Because of the nature of the material Tom possesses, we cannot let the location of that final base fall into their hands. Your job is to ensure that the material does not reach them. You are authorized to use any means necessary to protect it."

"Now, wait a minute!" said May. "I signed on to protect Tom, not to kill him!"

"Let me put this another way," said Dr. Kafka. "First, if this is what I think it is, then millions of people could die if you fail to do your duty—and only if there is no other way to protect that information. Secondly, if you don't, and the information falls into their hands, you will be tried and executed as a traitor."

"Well, I quit," said May. "I wasn't hired as an assassin."

"If that is your choice, then I am authorized to invoke Paragraph 48 of your contract, which allows me, under the War Powers Act, to place you in protective custody for the duration of this emergency. In other words, I can and will put you in a federal prison in isolation for as many years as we are in a state of war, or until the information is declassified. A simpler way of saying this is that you will be in jail for the rest of your life. Do you still wish to quit?"

"You bastard!" growled May. "You know my answer."

"Am I to assume that you wish to continue as Tom's bodyguard?" May nodded in agreement, barely controlling her anger.

"Good," replied Kafka. "Now go see Martha. She will help you learn to set up contact points in case you have to move Tom in a hurry. She will also give you a credit card that cannot be traced by others but will allow us to track you when you're on the move. Any questions? None? Good. You are dismissed. Now go see Martha."

As May stormed out, Kafka muttered under his breath, "Bastard is probably the nicest name I've been called this week."

Why me?

Outside Dr. Kafka's office, May worked through several mental relaxation techniques. Martha recognized the symptoms and waited until May was ready to listen.

"I see you got the good/bad, love-of-country speech," said Martha.

"You mean he treats others this way?" exclaimed May.

"Yes. In fact, I had the same speech several years back," said Martha.

"You did? Why?"

"I can't disclose everything, but suffice it to say that what we do here is so important that most nations would give up half of their national budgets to gain access to just a small percentage of this project. The reason we have had the success we've had is due to one man. You just came from his office."

"All I can say is that if this is his management style, then he needs to be replaced," said May.

"If you're with us for very long, you may reconsider that opinion. However, here are the three addresses. One is in California, and two are in Arizona. You can go into that room to memorize them. When you're finished, return the list to me, and I'll issue your credit card. In an emergency, you are to go to the nearest ATM machine and withdraw at least $1,000 to $2,000. Only do this once a day, and immediately put at least ten miles between you and the machine. Do not use the card at a store or for car rental. Save all your receipts; otherwise, those expenses will be deducted from your pay. Any questions?" asked Martha.

"I thought you couldn't withdraw more than $300 from any ATM," said May.

"Not with this card," said Martha. "Oh, yes, and if you lose it, let me know right away—I mean immediately. Anything else?" asked Martha. "If not, get started. Here's your list, and by the way, welcome aboard."

Chapter 10

The next morning, May collected the printouts from Tom's downloading. She was constantly amazed at the sheer volume of material being downloaded during each session. The single-spaced printouts often ranged between 5,000 and 10,000 pages, complete with graphics. These simultaneously filled several 50 GB high-density flash drives. May had to use a special sealed cart to transport the load to another level, where the drives were scanned by a computer for certain parameters—parameters that were strictly on a need-to-know basis and did not include her. The results were fed directly to Dr. Kafka's terminal at his desk. Dr. Kafka would then suggest which areas to explore next.

So far, the team was excited that the corruption rate in the data was significantly lower than what typically occurred when recording information onto a CD using a home computer. May had learned that much of the material was encoded to prevent unauthorized viewing by the "storage units." After several days, a great deal of information had been extracted, but not the specific information Dr. Kafka was looking for. On the third day, he made an extreme decision and ordered that the decoding procedures be downloaded directly into Tom's brain.

"You should be able to help us find what we're looking for once your brain assimilates the information," said Dr. Kafka.

"If this headache goes away, I might be able to understand what you're saying," replied Tom, holding his head.

"Take the rest of the day off," said Dr. Kafka. Then, turning to May, he added, "And, May, you stay with him just in case he needs something."

"Yes, sir," replied May. "Come on, Tom, let's get up to the infirmary and get something for that headache," she said, guiding Tom to a nearby wheelchair.

After the infirmary visit, May put Tom to bed, hoping he would recover from the treatment. As she watched him sleep, she tried to sort out what had transpired over the last few days—the special training with bizarre techniques, including blowguns, air rifles, boomerangs, knife throwing, and slingshots. She also remembered hearing snatches of conversations among the scientists about some of the information Tom carried. Could one person possess that much information without even knowing it? Shades of science fiction. Even Star Trek would feel right at home using this technique.

Dr. Kafka's attitude and insistence that she stay on the job was a strong negative. But the excitement of discovery seemed to win out, and she decided to stay anyway. Some of the other levels hinted at breakthroughs that were light-years beyond anything she had worked on at the university—even more advanced than the projects in labs sponsored by the military or CIA. She hoped she might eventually become a full-fledged member of the research team rather than just a glorified gofer for an old schoolteacher. He was kind of nice, though, in a fatherly way, and she enjoyed the late afternoon walks and quiet talks they shared about their lives.

Around then, her head drooped to her chest, and she fell asleep, helped along by a little sleeping gas monitored by the medical team. Dr. Ruth had suggested that both she and Tom would benefit from extra rest since they had been working 18-hour days for over three weeks.

Chapter 11

"That confirms it," said the dark-complexioned young man, looking through the powerful binoculars. "That truck drove into the shed loaded with those special chemicals. Now, it sits much higher on its springs. That shed must be an entrance to the facility. We must alert the rest of the teams and plan the attack as soon as possible."

"Agreed," said the young man lying on the sand next to him. He then spoke into a cell phone to arrange for all the leaders to meet at Point Freedom. Afterward, he destroyed the phone with a handy rock and buried it to prevent it from ever being used or traced.

The two men then carefully crawled down the side of the small gully and followed it to a ravine that headed southwest, where it ended at a dirt road. There, they uncovered a motorcycle concealed in a storm drain and drove back to their motel. At the motel, they collected their belongings and left in a nondescript, full-size pickup truck with the motorcycle loaded in the back.

Twenty minutes later, they pulled into a deserted rest stop where they left the motorcycle with the key in the ignition. Later that day, a teenager discovered the motorcycle and took it for a joyride. He eventually hid it in an abandoned toolshed in the desert.

The two men continued driving toward Barstow for the next hour. They turned onto Wylie Wells Road and drove to a small, isolated farmhouse. Pulling around to the backyard, they parked and went inside.

The living room appeared normal, outfitted with the latest furniture from the local Salvation Army surplus store. However, the bedrooms told a different story. In one, there was a sophisticated amateur radio communication setup. On the other, a large arsenal of assorted weapons was concealed under the floor in a specially built vault.

The antenna on the roof was disguised as one of several digital satellite dishes. It linked to an older Soviet spy satellite, where transmissions were rebroadcast either down over the western United States or bounced to an Arab satellite to be beamed to headquarters. Naturally, all transmissions were encrypted.

The two men walked into the communication room and warmed up the Kenwood transceiver.

"Hurry up, Allie. I want to check out the system before the others get here." "Give me a minute," said Allie, twiddling with the dial and pushing several buttons. "See, I told you it would work," said Allie, pointing to the 17-inch flat-screen monitor connected to the radio showing the shed they had just observed several hours ago.

"You said that amateur stuff wouldn't work. Surprise. All I needed was to have the uplink close enough to receive the signal. Now we can watch TV in the shed at the same time. Isn't technology wonderful?"

Allie had packaged the Kenwood fast scan camera with a solar charging panel and switcher in a small box disguised as a rock. He beamed the signal at a hill several miles away, where he concealed another transmitter and solar panel, this time pointed at the Soviet satellite in geosynchronous orbit. They could watch the shed for up to 12 hours before the system would have to shut down to recharge the battery. They could also remotely turn on and off the system. A zoom lens in a small, two-axis motor drive adopted from an amateur telescope drive allowed them to move the camera 45° left or right and up or down. Allie was talking faster and faster as he warmed to his subject.

Why me?

"Enough already," said Mohammed, who had heard this talk several times already. "Let's just see if it will hold together for the next 36 hours. I am going to lie down. Call me when the others arrive."

By car, truck, and motorcycle, the team leaders began to arrive. Once all seven were present, Mohammed began without a preamble.

"We found it! Now, here's how we'll take it." He displayed a map of the area, created by their scouts. "This is where we'll converge. There doesn't appear to be any protection other than a chain-link fence—no doubt to keep the curiosity of the locals to a minimum."

"Much to our benefit," chuckled one leader, who was responsible for breaching the outer defenses.

"We now have the area under video surveillance, thanks to one of Allie's gorgeous gadgets," said the leader, glancing at Allie, who beamed at the compliment. The leader continued, "There should be no problem getting past the fence. What about the shed? Do we have any intel on getting in?"

"Obviously, everything is underground, as far as we can tell. There appears to be a standard card key system, which shouldn't pose a problem once we attack. We simply acquire one from someone who will no longer need it," said another leader, a woman.

"Once inside, we can expect some resistance. But if we reach the control center, likely located on a lower level, we'll have access to everything. Mohammed will install a tap on any computer we find and download all the data using repeater transmitters placed strategically here and here," the leader said, pointing to the elevator shaft.

"The information will then be relayed to the computers at home for analysis. Once that's done, we'll leave and regroup at the Rhonda assembly area. If there's a Coke can taped to the post holding the city limits sign, proceed to the next rally point: Synagogue. These rally points are known only to you, so keep it that way."

"Lori, you're the one who secured the information. After the attack, the Americans will start reviewing everyone who talked to anyone. Your name will come up. Using their advanced technology, they'll undoubtedly locate a picture of you, making it easier for them to track us down. The same goes for anyone whose face is exposed during the attack. There must be nothing that helps them find us."

Why me?

Mohammed's tone became fervent. "Comrades, our day is almost upon us. The day when our small sting will topple the giant, and by Allah's will, it will become a reality very soon!"

With those words, the group broke into subgroups to study and refine their earlier plans for attacking the lab.

Chapter 12

The day of the attack was a normal Sunday for the lab. Nothing unusual happened during the day except for some teenagers' joyriding on their Hondas with their girlfriends, who were wearing very little—except helmets.

"Looks like they'll be getting some today," said the gate guard. "I wish I were with them."

If the guard had stopped the kids, he would have noticed that the helmets the girls wore had small holes cut in the sides, allowing helmet cams to record and transmit pictures to a temporary command center set up in a truck parked along the state road near the area the two young men had visited the day before. In the truck, the leader monitored the pictures and communicated with female radio operators. When he confirmed that everything was the same as before, he spoke one word on the radio that connected him to various teams.

"Jihad!"

With that word, he activated the next phase of the plan. The motorcycle riders rode to a small nearby shed, where they changed into black SWAT-type clothing purchased at several local Army-Navy stores. The automatic weapons and explosives were taken from the supply at the command house. They then waited.

That evening, the scheduled supply truck showed up slightly late and without the usual radio call upon approaching the lab's final mile. This violated protocol, as any break in routine required notification to the chief base security officer, who would notify Kafka and place the base on a yellow alert. The guard on duty delayed activating the alert by two minutes too long. He misjudged the truck's speed in the twilight, and by the time he realized his mistake, the truck had torn through the gate.

Two shots from the men on the passenger side of the truck eliminated the guard just after he hit the alarm button. The truck continued to the shed two hundred yards beyond the gate. Following behind the truck were the motorcyclists, no longer looking like innocent teenagers but rather like the well-trained commandos they were.

As the truck pulled up to the shed, one of the people in the back jumped out, ran to the shed door, slapped a Semtex charge over the lock, and jumped to the side before pressing the button on the transmitter. The explosion did little to the door or the lock. That's when the terrorists discovered that the shed was a heavily reinforced blockhouse disguised to look like an old equipment shed.

"Shit," muttered the explosives expert, who then ran to the back of the truck, retrieved a large satchel charge, and placed it beside the door, warning everyone to pull around to the side of the shed. When they were clear, she pulled the lanyard and ran to join the others. The explosion blew open the door and sent a shock wave down to the first level to announce their presence. "So much for surprise," muttered the leader as the explosion shook his truck parked on the freeway a mile away on a dirt road.

Automatic alarms went off on all levels. Kafka, who was having dinner in the executive dining room with his assistant, was barely able to beat her to the door and down the hall to the stairwell. At the Command Center, they rapidly activated the security grid. Then, they saw several persons in black ski masks guarding the inside of the shed through the concealed cameras hidden on the outside level by shipping and receiving. The elevator indicator showed it had just reached the second-level landing. The camera inside the elevator just had time to show a number of black-suited individuals, all the same size and height, before they spotted the camera and shot it out.

Why me?

"Seal the lab," said Dr. Kafka.

"Yes sir," said his assistant, flipping a red cover-up and pushing the button underneath.

Immediately, the elevator locked up, the doors in the stairwell locked, and the titanium-steel shutters dropped around the Command Center. Now the only way around the lab was with a special card that could only open the doors when the Command Center had verified who was using the card.

"John, what's your status?" asked Dr. Kafka.

"My board shows they are attacking only the shipping shed. It appears there are about 20 to 30 of them. I'm sending two-thirds of my men to meet them on level four, keeping the others in reserve in case of an attack from another entrance."

"Sounds good," replied Dr. Kafka. "Get the packages ready to move if necessary."

"Aye-aye, sir," said the security chief, betraying his Navy SEAL background. Pressing another key, Kafka said, "Doctors, you'd best wake up our sleeping beauties just in case they need to leave."

Turning to his assistant, he added, "Contact Bill and have him stand by at the dude ranch entrance, just in case."

"Yes, sir," replied the ex-Air Force Major.

Dr. Kafka went into his office and typed a failsafe command into his computer. This command would erase all the lab's memory banks in less than an hour if the counter-command wasn't entered. The data was secure, as it was transmitted via a secure satellite to NASA storage facilities in Virginia on an hourly basis.

He lifted his phone and heard, "Johnson."

"Pyramid, condition red. We count 20 to 30 inside the facility. Your ETA?"

"Twenty-five to thirty minutes," replied Brigadier General Sam Johnson, commander of the Marine base at El Toro.

"Very well," said Kafka, pressing an orange button on his phone. The White House duty officer nearly dropped his phone when he heard the words: Thunder, condition red, priority alpha.

"Yes, sir," the officer said, connecting Kafka to the President.

Why me?

T"Hello," said President Smith. "What can I do for you?"

"Mr. President, we are under attack by unknown forces. We currently count 20 to 30 inside the facility. The Marine base has been notified and is en route."

"Very well. Keep me informed," said the President, advising the Secret Service as he headed to the situation room.

Meanwhile, Kafka checked back with his assistant. "How far have they gotten?"

"They've reached the labs. Reinforcements must have come down the elevator shaft. I counted at least 8 to 10 who got past our defenses," the assistant replied.

Kafka pressed another button. "How does it look from your view?"

"They've bypassed my men. I've committed reserves to slow them down until the Marines arrive. ETA?"

"Eighteen to twenty minutes at best," said Kafka.

"That's too long," said the chief. "These guys are good and getting reinforcements. I suggest a scramble."

"I concur. Can you hold them long enough to evacuate the others?"

"Probably," said the chief.

Kafka flipped another switch and announced over the PA, "All personnel. This is a firestorm order. I repeat: this is not a drill. The countdown has started."

"What the hell is firestorm?" asked Mohammed, one of the intruders.

."I don't know," replied team leader three. "But we're getting reports of people trying to escape. One man was yelling something about 'get out before it's activated.' Unfortunately, he died before explaining further."

"Have you found the computer?"

"We are setting the charges as we speak," said team leader three.

The leader heard explosions in the background.

"We are into the Command Center!" came the triumphant announcement.

The terrorist team quickly reconnoitered the area and found the computer controls. One bomb expert carefully opened the cabinet.

Why me?

"There appear to be no booby traps. I'm going to insert the tap."

After he concealed the tap within the case and tested the connection, he carefully put everything back the way it was.

"Okay, let's get out of here," said the team leader. "Put any stuff you find in this backpack."

The group members quickly deposited their findings into the sack, collected their weapons, and started out the door.

"Firestorm has been activated," came over the complex's PA system. "Firestorm will activate in two minutes."

"I don't like the sound of that. Let's get out of here," yelled the team leader as he charged down the hallway.

Halfway down the hall, the team leader disappeared in an explosion of shrapnel. His body was literally divided into four parts by the force of the blast in such an enclosed space. The woman behind him would never recover her sanity, even after physically healing, as she had seen parts of her leader's head smashing into her face, while several pieces of shrapnel would prevent her from ever conceiving. The other three cell members made it to the stairwell, dragging the wounded woman. There, they took out the person who tossed a grenade, the janitor. The other two people made it to the outside and joined the six others who had gotten out. Just then, it seemed someone lit up the whole area from below. Flame was released into each corridor, effectively reducing to ash anyone in the corridors. Unfortunately, several workers, along with eight or 10 of the terrorists, didn't make it to the safe areas. Fortunately, their pain was very short.

The eight remaining terrorists scrambled to find transportation. Three of them rode out on a single motorcycle, and four others escaped in the truck, heading to the staging area where each of them left using their prearranged transportation.

The eighth person attempted to flee on foot but was captured by the Marines, who literally dived on him from their helicopter. Tragically, he managed to activate the suicide vest he had been wearing, succeeding in blowing himself up and injuring three Marines as well as damaging one of the helicopters.

Chapter 13

While everyone was having fun, the medics flushed out the air flowing into the rooms where Tom and May were sleeping. They then ran into their rooms and dragged the sleepers out. Tom was halfway down the hall before he realized he was awake.

"Just thought it was a dream," he would later recount.

May woke up faster but was just as confused until the run up the first three flights of stairs cleared out her lungs and got the blood flowing to her brain.

"What's happening?" she asked as they began climbing the third flight of steps.

"We've been attacked," yelled the senior medic. "You have to get Tom to a safe place. There's a car waiting up top. The driver will take you wherever you want. After he drops you off, go to your pickup point and follow your training from there. If Tom starts acting funny, give him one blue capsule to quiet him down if necessary. If he's in danger of being captured, give him the yellow capsule," the medic said, handing her a small envelope.

They were approaching the first floor when they saw the assistant holding a very authoritative Sig Sauer 9 mm machine gun. When she saw them, she motioned for them to stop just below the landing.

"Let me go check to see if it's still clear," she said.

While she was checking, May turned to the medic and said, "Doc, we just ran up nine flights of steps with you and the other medic practically carrying us. Yet you look like it was nothing."

The doctor gave a little chuckle as he shifted a 9 mm Glock from inside his lab coat that May hadn't noticed before.

"In my other life, it probably would've been the warm-up before we did some real exercise in the Army Rangers. The medics had to take the same training as regular soldiers to keep up with them during an operation."

"No kidding, Doc. You were a Ranger?" she asked.

"Lt. Col. Tom Handel, retired, at your service, Ma'am," said the doctor, giving her a mock salute.

Before she could ask anything else, the assistant returned and said, "It's clear for the moment, so you'd best get moving. The car is just coming around the corner. Act naturally as you walk out to it. Get in, and the driver will get you outta here."

"Let's go," said the Doc, half-carrying May out the door, pretending to be holding her arm like a good friend would. Tom was still shaking and groggy, so the other medic treated him like he was drunk, speaking to him like a friend who'd had too much to drink—just in case someone was watching.

The medics got them into the taxi. As the Doc was shutting the door, he whispered, "Good luck and God bless. The fate of our country may be resting in that man's head."

Chapter 14

As the taxi pulled away, the sky behind them briefly lit up with the results of the firestorm.

"The spin doctors will be busy," said the driver as he gunned the engine, and the taxi dashed onto the road.

"Will you guys watch out the back and sides for anybody that looks unfriendly while I concentrate on driving?" said the driver as he accelerated to racing speed.

"What does an unfriendly look like?" asked Tom.

"Somebody pointing something at us, like a rocket launcher or a big gun," grunted the driver as he took a corner on two wheels and a prayer.

After about five minutes at high speed, the driver slowed down to just below the sound barrier so as not to attract attention. As he pulled onto the access road and began accelerating up to freeway speed, they missed the two people hiding in the wash beside their motorcycles. One of the girls activated her helmet camera and transmitted the picture to the control center with the commentary that the taxi was coming from the target area at a high rate of speed.

Why me?

In the van, the terrorist leader looked at the picture and decided, "If that's somebody leaving the facility through another way, then they might be important," he thought, flipping a cell phone switch.

"Team seven, check out the taxi headed your way. Detain the passengers for further questioning," he quietly said.

The response was two short clicks for "Roger."

Once the cab turned onto the highway, they all breathed a collective sigh.

"It looks like we made it," said Tom to the other two occupants.

"Let's not count our chickens yet," said the driver as he moved the speedometer up to 85 mph.

"What did you do to this taxi?" asked Tom. "It's much quieter and smoother than the one I rode in."

"After the cheapskates paid me, I got it tuned up," said the driver, mentally crossing his fingers. In reality, he had a device that could be turned on or off to make a whole lot of noise like an old, out-of-tune engine.

Then, as they flew past a big rock on the side of the road, a set of flashing red lights appeared in the rearview mirror.

"I can't believe this. A cop in this section of the road? As many times as I've driven this road, I've never seen a single cop of any kind along here. It's too hot in the daytime and too far away from Doughnut King at night."

"Then maybe it's not," said May. "Let's be on our toes."

As the motorcycle cop pulled up alongside the cab and motioned them over, May yelled, "Get out of here. It's a trap!"

At that point, the "cop" pulled out a very unofficial .44 Mag Desert Storm automatic and began firing at the tires.

"He's in for a surprise," said the driver. "Those are puncture-proof tires."

At that point, the officer seemed to hear them and began firing at the driver.

"Don't worry," said the driver as a series of small flowers appeared on his side window from the shots. "Those windows are bulletproof. But I think it's time to stop playing with him," said the driver as he pushed a button on the dashboard.

Suddenly, a wide stream of clear synthetic oil shot from under the rear bumper. When the motorcyclist realized what it was, it was too late, and he went sailing over the curb and down the side of a gully. Fortunately for the cop, he separated from the bike before it hit a boulder and burst into flames. He landed, breaking his neck and many bones in his body before finishing a violent cartwheel in the desert.

The police were at least able to identify the remains and return them to his homeland for burial.

Tom and May watched the light from the motorcycle exploding against the rock in a small fireball.

"Nice call on the fake cop. How did you know he was a fake?" asked Tom.

"Most motorcycle cops have their helmets connected to the radio, but this guy was talking into a cell phone."

"Good call, but bad news," said the driver. "If he was talking to someone, then he may have alerted them to our direction. So, we'll have to change our plans a bit."

With that, he turned off at the next exit and pulled onto a parallel road, cutting in toward a nearby town via a back route. On the outskirts of Lancaster, they came upon a deserted Bank of America ATM where, following instructions, May pulled out $2,000. The driver then called a local rental car company on a burner cell phone and reserved a Mustang convertible since it was the only car available for the next morning.

"That's fine," said May, "but morning is 12 hours away. What are we going to do until then?"

"I don't know about you, but I am going to sleep," said the driver.

"Yeah… where?" asked May.

"Give me a minute," said the driver.

He turned a couple of corners, smiled, and pointed.

"Over there," he said.

He was pointing at a large, gated apartment complex.

"How are you going to get in?" asked May. "It's gated."

"So what?" said the driver. "Just wait."

He pulled over to the side of the entry gate and waited until a car approached. As soon as the driver activated the gate, he pulled in behind the other car and drove through.

"Piece of cake," said the driver as he pulled into a parking space in the back of the complex.

The driver got out and opened the trunk. He took out a couple of blankets and a small bag. He handed out the blankets and some MRE meal packets. Then he produced Styrofoam cups and poured a round of coffee from the large thermos he pulled out of the bag.

"This would be fun if we only had a bathroom," said Tom. "Us old folks can't get too far from the restroom. I'd use the bushes, but I'm a bit worried someone might see me, and I'd get arrested for public indecency."

"Don't worry," said the driver. "Over by the pool, there are bathrooms and showers open all night."

"How do you know that?" asked May. "They usually close those places to key only."

"In most places, that would be true. However, this is a local singles apartment complex. People get a hankering to go skinny-dipping at all hours and often forget to bring their keys, so management leaves it open all night."

"How do you know that?" asked May.

"I used to date a girl who lived here. Also, the security is only on call at night because management got tired of bailing out tenants for indecent exposure. And before you get too nosy, you both need to get as much sleep as possible.

Tomorrow will be a long day. Just to show you what a good guy I am, I'll take the first watch. May, take the second, and Tom, you take the last watch."

The next morning, a very noisy blower run by the lawn maintenance person blasted Tom awake. He looked around, trying to figure out where he was.

"Was this all a dream or what?" he wondered aloud.

"Hello, Sleeping Beauty," he heard from the front seat.

"You let me sleep through my watch," he said.

"The way you were snoring, it was impossible to sleep. Besides, you needed it."

"Thanks. I did need it. I owe you."

"Don't worry; I'll collect," said May.

"By the way, where is our chauffeur?" asked Tom.

"He's checking out the bathroom and will be back soon. Before he gets back, let me review our itinerary. If something happens to me, you are to report to the Greyhound Bus station at Needles, California. Dial eight 5's on the middle payphone. I know that normal phone numbers are only seven digits long, but that's why you have to use the middle payphone. Follow the directions, and they should bring you in."

"I know, I know," said Tom before May could protest. "This is just in case because I plan on being there with you. Dr K owes me a lot of money and I intend on collecting it."

"Good to see you're awake," the driver said, walking up to the car. "Are you ready for some food?"

It was then that Tom noticed a loud rumbling—not from his stomach, but May's.

"I guess that means yes," said the driver, and they all laughed.

They had breakfast at the Golden Arches and picked up some salads to take with them for later. Then they stopped by a different ATM, where May withdrew another $2,000. She handed the cash to Tom and said, "Since I've got the card, I'll use my money first in case we get separated."

The driver gave a small nod of approval as they continued their preparations. Before dropping them off at the rental car location, he reached under the passenger seat and retrieved a hidden compartment containing several items. "Take what you think you'll need," he said, gesturing at the weapons and gear.

Tom leaned in and picked up a Smith & Wesson .357 Magnum with Pachmayr grips and night sights. He added a box each of .38 Special and .357 Magnum ammo to his selection. May chose a 9 mm Springfield Armory XD auto, two extra clips, and two boxes of special armor-piercing rounds that were not available to the general public. Finally, she grabbed a Cold Steel Tanto blade with a fitted sheath, designed to secure the knife in any position. "For a lab assistant, you sure know a lot about weapons," Tom remarked with a grin.

"I had two brothers and a father in the military," May replied. "Their idea of fun was holding field-stripping contests, mixing the parts of at least two weapons while blindfolded. The loser had to do dishes for a week. In four years, I had to do dishes three times." She smiled, clearly proud of her skill.

At the rental car agency, everything went smoothly, thanks to the IDs that the driver had previously prepared for them. The clerk handed them the keys to a Mustang convertible—the only vehicle available that day. Before they left, they purchased a map of California, Nevada, and Arizona from the office. Tom casually asked the clerk how long it would take to get to Needles.

May almost fainted when he made that slip in asking directions and giving their destination. She let him know in no uncertain terms what she thought of his stupid, dumbass slip. Properly chastised, Tom drove the first two hours.

Chapter 15

At the end of two hours, Tom stopped the car for gas and coffee at a 7-11 store. After he topped off the tank, May insisted on driving.

"I'm the better driver, and you need to rest and hopefully let your mind decode some more so you'll be ready when we get where we're going."

The drive to Needles was uneventful and pleasant. Both people, while somewhat lost in their own feelings about last night, failed to notice a small commuter plane that seemed to be following the road rather than a prescribed flight plan. But it was soon out of sight, leaving Tom and May to enjoy the sun and the freedom of the open road.

The plane reached Needles about an hour and a half before May and Tom. The pilot stayed with the plane, and the four passengers rented two SUVs at the local rental agency by the airport. They headed out onto the interstate. Soon, they spotted their quarry coming toward them in the opposite lane. Unfortunately, the local speed trap forced them to drive around the bend and down two miles before they could turn around. They also had to slow down to avoid attracting attention. The net result was that Tom and May got to Needles before the terrorists.

In Needles, Tom and May spotted a local shopping mall and pulled into the huge parking lot where they could hide their car in the crowd of vehicles. They blended in with the crowds of shoppers to ensure their anonymity. Inside the mall, they had dinner at the Hometown Buffet.

After finally getting turned in the right direction, one of the terrorists' cars raced ahead, trying to catch up with Tom and May. Meanwhile, the pilot fueled his aircraft and took off to help in the search. The other car drove more sedately, frequently checking with the plane overhead.

"I think I see something in the mall parking lot off to your left," radioed the pilot. "Not sure because they must be having a hell of a sale. It looks like most of the town is parked there."

Once in the parking lot, the terrorists spotted the red convertible that matched the license plate from the rental agency.

The leader decided to split into teams. Your team will divide up and enter from each end of the mall, and the driver will watch the convertible.

"If you spot them, let us know so we can corner them in the parking lot," said the leader.

Inside the mall, Tom and May stopped at the local Sears store to pick up some basic clothes and jackets, including two backpacks to put their stuff in. Then, they stopped at the Rite Aid to get a few of the basic toiletries they would need for the trip. As they were walking out, May grabbed Tom's arm and said,

"Stop here and look into the window."

As Tom turned to the window of a sporting goods store, May appeared to be pointing at a pair of boots but was instead pointing at the reflection of two men just coming through the door.

"See those two men coming through the door?" asked May. "They don't fit in with the rest of the crowd around here. They look to be military, and they sure are looking at everybody very carefully. Let's duck in here and watch them from inside. It's a little too open out here."

Chapter 16

Inside the sporting goods store, Tom and May moved to behind a showcase containing air rifles.

"Where did they go?" asked Tom.

"I thought that they were by the door, but I don't see them at all."

"You don't have to look very far," said May. "One of them just came into the store. He's over by the camping gear, looking around."

"Where's the other one?" whispered Tom.

"I lost him when we ducked in here," said May.

Outside, the other terrorist was talking on a cell phone to the leader.

"I think we found them. They are in the sporting goods store at the end of the mall. Ahmed has gone in to find them."

"Very good," replied the leader. "We will create a diversion to get them out of the mall. You stand back up in the middle. We will be ready to go in 15 minutes."

Inside the store, Tom and May were both moving while trying to keep display racks and shelving between them and the terrorist.

"Why don't we just duck out and leave?" asked Tom.

"Because the other one is out there covering the only way out of here," said May.

Tom replied, "There's got to be a backdoor for deliveries."

"Great," said May. "Why didn't I think of that?"

As they carefully made their way past the showcase of guns, knives, specialized camping gear, dehydrated food, and climbing gear, there was a thumping sound, and the lights went out. As a few emergency lights came on, Tom and May found themselves ducked down next to the showcase of knives.

"Where is he?"

"Who?" said Tom.

"The one that was trying to find us," replied May.

In the dimness of the emergency light and in the confusion, it was hard to see anything. That was until a soft "pop" shattered the case in front of them.

"He's over there," said Tom. "We've got to get past him," yelled Tom.

May dropped her packages and grabbed the Marine K-Bar knife from the shattered case, stood up, and hurled it at the terrorist just rounding the corner of a rack of books about 20 feet away. The knife caught him in the right eye, passing through the eyeball and lodging in that portion of the brain that controls motor function. The net result was for the terrorists to suddenly go limp and collapse.

"Let's go!" yelled May, grabbing Tom by the arm and dragging him toward the front door.

Just then, another shot shattered the case next to them, and the ricochet hit a small girl held in her father's arms. Fortunately, the girl had on a backpack containing several schoolbooks, thus saving her life, although nobody would notice a hole in her pack until the next day. Several other shots hit around them but didn't find their marks.

"We're trapped!" yelled Tom. "We've got to get out of here before he gets reinforcements or learns how to shoot. He's got us pinned down, in case you haven't noticed," yelled May.

"We've got to distract him. He's too far away to throw anything," said May, "and I can't get a clear shot from here."

"What is a PCP rifle?"

"He's not too far for this," said Tom.

"What's that, a slingshot? And I can't get a clear shot from here with this air rifle," exclaimed May.

"Yes," said Tom. "I should be able to distract him with this. Can you get him from here?"

"With what?" exclaimed May. "All I can reach are these BB guns."

"Those aren't BB guns. They are air rifles. Many have the same power, caliber, and accuracy as a .22 rifle," whispered Tom as he picked up one of the rifles from the broken case and grabbed a tin of pellets and darts. He just barely got his hand back from the case in time as another shot hit where his hand had been.

"This is a Beeman air rifle. It cocks like this, and you insert the pellet or dart here. Can you handle it from here? It shoots just like a regular rifle—no kick, little noise. The effective range is about 50 yards. Will that work?"

"Not with a .22," said May. "I need to stop him so he can't warn the others. Wait a minute. I have something that may do it. Hand me one of those darts. See if you can hit that light or glass fixture behind him with that slingshot."

Tom picked up a small bottle of water purification tablets and shot it in a near-perfect shot that hit just near the shooter, causing him to rise and look toward the noise. May then shot him in the side of the neck. The man slapped his neck and collapsed.

"Let's go!" yelled May as they dashed for the rear of the store.

"What did you shoot him with?" yelled Tom.

"You don't collapse like that from just a single dart."

"I rubbed it in something I found in a first-aid kit inside the broken showcase."

What she didn't say was that she had used saliva to dissolve the little yellow pill from the pack that the doctor gave her to use on Tom to prevent him from falling into the wrong hands. The pill caused a shutdown of the brain and heart, as the terrorist found out when he pulled the dart out of his neck and was dead before he hit the floor.

Outside, confusion reigned. People were standing around, and fire trucks and police were arriving. Tom and May made it to the car, only to find the other driver waiting for them.

"Infidel! Whore!" yelled the man as he snapped off a shot at her.

The shot grazed May on the side. Tom yelled and threw a small backpack shovel he was carrying. It struck the terrorist in the throat, almost decapitating him.

"Are you okay?" yelled Tom as he shoved May into the backseat of their convertible, jumped into the driver's side, started the car, and recklessly threaded his way out of the parking lot. On the way out, there was a pinging sound in the back of the car. Tom drove at the speed limit until he reached the freeway. Two hours later, he pulled into a motel. Helping May into the room, Tom laid her gently on the bed.

"Now let's see what the damage is," he said as he carefully unbuttoned her blouse.

"Ouch, that must've hurt, but it's just a flesh wound. Hold this towel on it, and I'll be back shortly."

"Wait," said May.

"We need to get some money, so here's the card, and the code is 608242. Remember to go at least ten miles away from here."

"Got it," said Tom.

Tom left the motel and drove to an ATM on the other side of town. Following the procedure outlined by May, he got the money, then stopped by a super drugstore where he purchased an expedition first aid kit and some antibiotics. On the way back, he caught a local radio newscast reporting an incident at the mall.

"There appears to have been a gang shootout in the sporting goods store," the announcer said. "The police are looking for a red convertible that was driven by two people wanted for questioning."

"That's not good," thought Tom. "Here I am driving a red convertible in a redneck town. I've got to get rid of this car," he thought as he pulled into an alley. Taking the money and other items, he put up the top, left the keys in the ignition, and walked down the alley to a parking lot, where he spied a used car lot about two blocks down. At the lot, he told the salesman he needed a car for his mother-in-law, who lived out in the desert. Tom finally got a used Cherokee for $2000. He had to give his home address that matched up with his driver's license.

Back at the motel, Tom found May passed out on the bed. She was exhausted, and for that matter, so was he. But he had one more thing to do before he could rest. He gave May some oral antibiotics and sewed up her wound.

"For a teacher, you sure know a lot about trauma treatment," murmured May.

"I didn't," said Tom. "But apparently, that information is part of the database I was given. The action caused the needed information to surface."

With that, he dressed her wound, covered her, and lay down beside her, asleep before his head hit the pillow.

Chapter 17

The next morning, Tom was awakened by a knocking on the door.

"Room service," called the maid.

Tom quickly went to the door and stopped her just before she could see who was in the room.

"We'll be checking out at noon, so please come back then," he said.

"Gracias," said the maid as she pushed her cart toward the next room.

"You always show a date this kind of excitement?" came a voice from the bed.

"No, usually a better time, but only on the second date," Tom replied.

That brought a chuckle from the figure on the bed.

"How do you feel?" Tom asked.

"My side hurts like hell, but I'll live," said May.

"Good," said Tom, "because we have to get out of here."

He told her about the newscast and his decision to buy another car.

May asked Tom how he felt, and he replied, "Every bone and joint in my body hurts, so we'll have to be sharing the aspirin bottle for a while."

"So much for the strong macho type," May teased.

"Listen," said Tom, "at my age, I've earned the right to complain. Fortunately, those exercise classes really helped. Otherwise, I'd probably still be back at the mall, trying to catch my breath. I suspect you could use some liniment yourself."

"Pretty good guess," said May, "but I still have a tube of the liniment Dr. Handell gave me back at the lab. It's in my backpack along with the other stuff we bought. If you'd be so gallant as to hand it to me, please."

Tom did as she asked and helped her apply the liniment to her back. May returned the gesture by rubbing it on his back.

"That stuff is really good," said Tom. "When we finish this gig, I'm going to buy a case of it. Between my wife and me, we go through a lot of liniment."

Before they checked out, they cleaned up the room so the maid wouldn't suspect anything. Tom managed to "borrow" several towels and washcloths from the maid's cart while she was cleaning the neighboring room to replace the bloodied ones from the night before. They disposed of the soiled towels in the dumpster out back.

May insisted on driving to familiarize herself with the car. They stopped for gas and withdrew more money from an ATM inside a truck stop about an hour outside of town. Afterward, Tom took over driving because May wanted to study the map. Tom suspected the real reason was that she was still tired from her wound and needed rest.

Their next checkpoint was the bus station in Reno, Nevada. There, May contacted Dr. K and received directions for the next part of their trip. Dr. K explained that it would be safer for them to continue traveling as they were, but he would send a second car to meet them just outside the next town to act as an escort. He also arranged for a doctor to be on board to check on May.

Since they had time to kill while waiting for the backup team, Tom suggested they spend it at a nearby casino. The food was excellent, and they ate with gusto at the oyster bar.

A bucket of clams turned into two buckets, along with a variety of other seafood.

"So, this is what it's like to be on the government dole," Tom said, grinning, between bites of baked salmon and sips of a wonderful white wine.

After their meal, on the way out, Tom stopped by a quarter slot machine and dropped in four coins. He hit the jackpot!

The quarters clattered into the tray, the sound seemingly endless. Then, a guard arrived and escorted them to the cashier to collect the rest of their winnings. In total, they walked away with over $1,000. The casino took their picture for the winners' wall. They couldn't refuse without arousing suspicion, but they both agreed not to bet or gamble again while in Nevada.

Outside of town, Tom and May met the backup team. The same doctor from the ranch checked May over and pronounced her fit to continue. He gave her an antibiotic, a tetanus shot, and another tube of liniment, just to be safe.

The team also provided the duo with fresh clothing for the outdoors, untraceable cell phones, and a fresh supply of weapons.

Why me?

Once everyone was ready, they returned to their cars and set off. To avoid drawing attention, the backup team agreed to follow Tom and May at a distance of about a mile.

After several hours of driving, the group stopped for dinner at a small, local restaurant just off the highway, about a mile from the main road near a campground. They parked their cars in the side lot, facing outward for an easy exit.

Chapter 18

As the group walked around the restaurant, Dr. Kafka assigned one of the agents to stand guard by the cars. If anyone asked, he could say he was looking for some paperwork for the group inside.

"Don't worry. We'll get you a 'to-go meal.' How do you like your steak?"

Inside, while small, the place was spotless and decorated in an old western motif. Translation: items salvaged from local yard sales and an occasional piece standing by the curb waiting for the garbage pickup. The four tables with chairs surrounded the small three-stool counter.

The oilcloth table covers had the traditional red and white checkerboard design that matched Joan's apron when she came out to take the orders. She gave each table one menu that had several items marked out with a Magic Marker.

"We're out of those items, but the rest are available," she said by way of explanation.

The choices left were either a hamburger, a hot dog, or a steak and an undefined homemade soup of the day.

"What's the soup of the day?" asked Tom.

"I had some shrimp left over from last night's meal, so I made a shrimp bisque. I can give you a little sample to help you make up your mind."

"No thanks," said Tom.

"I'll just have the steak, medium rare, mashed potatoes."

"I'm out of mashed potatoes, but I can whip you up a good pile of home fries," said Joan.

"Sounds good," said Tom.

"I'll have the steak medium rare and anything else you want to put on the plate," said May.

"Hey, leave some for the rest of us," said Dr. K.

"Why, I'm just a growing girl," quirked May, "and please save me a piece of that chocolate pie your husband was bragging about outside."

The rest of the group ordered pretty much the same combination since that was basically all that was available. Dr. Kafka commented after the meal that it was one of the finest meals he'd ever had. The steaks were as tender as any Kobe beef he had had, the bisque was out of heaven, and the pie was to die for.

"If I didn't already have a first-class cook, assuming he's still alive, I would kidnap that woman and lock her in a kitchen with unlimited resources. She is awesome."

The team later found out that Joan had been an executive chef for one of the top restaurants in Houston, Texas. She was also a rated Cordon Bleu chef from New Orleans. She came out here to the campground to get away from the stress and pressure of being one of the top-rated chefs in the United States. Outside, Dr. Kafka sent one of the team members back to get a gallon of that wonderful chicory coffee as an after-dessert drink. He also noticed that behind the restaurant was a fairly large campground. It had some cabins and didn't seem very full. He asked the cook who ran it and where was the office.

"Outside around the back of the restaurant is the office. You can check if they have any vacancies."

When he went outside and around back, Dr. Kafka saw a small "office" sign over a door. Inside the small room, Joan came out from the back door and said, "How can I help you, gentlemen?"

Why me?

Dr. Kafka started laughing and playing along and asked, "Do you have any vacancies?"

"For how many?" asked Joan.

"Ten," said Dr. Kafka. May looked at him and started to say only seven but kept quiet.

Dr. Kafka said, "We have three more that will be late arrivals."

Elaine looked Dr. Kafka up and down and said, "That will be $800 per night and includes breakfast."

"We're just a family headed out on vacation. How about a discount? "Some family," said Joan.

"You all are packing enough iron. I was afraid I would have to reinforce the floor to keep it from collapsing. Isn't that right, Honey?"

"Right," said a disemboweled voice.

May said, "You're mistaken. We're just a family out on vacation. You are carrying a Ruger Max 9 in a belly holster and a Ruger LCR in your right pocket. The lady next to you has a 9 mm Glock 17 and one clip, plus a boot knife. The man next to her has a 357 Smith and Wesson plus two boxes of ammo in his fanny pack. Shall I go on? One other thing:

there are enough weapons in your cars to start a small war. If you try something, it probably won't go well for you all."

With that, they heard a click and turned just in time to see bars slide over the small window and door. With another click, a bullet-proof plexiglass sheet rose from the desk in front of Joan, effectively sealing off the back of the room and protecting her.

"Who the hell are you?" yelled Dr. Kafka.

"Occasionally we get some motorcycle gangs and other groups that want to take advantage of our hospitality. So, we return the favor. Now you have one minute to prove why we should not gas you and save you for a friend of ours."

Dr. Kafka looked around the stunned group and then said, "We're a government group on a classified mission."

"Please prove it," said the disemboweled voice.

"Call this number," said Dr. Kafka, "and ask for an extension Echo Charlie Hotel One."

"That's the White House," said the voice.

"How the hell did you know that, and who the hell are you? You're obviously not just a mom-and-pop operation. Which agency are you?" exclaimed Dr. Kafka.

"Wait," said the voice. In the silence, May mentally got ready to fight.

Suddenly, the voice said, "You check out, Dr. Kafka, by the President, no less. He also said Echo, Echo, 1942 and that if you were captured this easily, he might have to find a bodyguard for you in your present senile state."

Everybody turned to look at Dr. Kafka, whose face was red enough to cook a steak.

"That's enough," said Joan.

"Quit playing around with our guests." As the wall retracted and the door unlocked, she turned to look at Dr. Kafka and said," That's just Dan, my husband. He does like to show off his toys." She went on to say, "We are a full-service, secure, 24/7 conference center. If you need anything, just press zero on the phone. If you need a secure phone, Dan will take you to one and provide the privacy you may want. Anything else? Then please enjoy your stay. Included are some cookies you all may need for tonight."

She reached under the counter and handed two bags of cookies to Dr. Kafka. "Oh, yes. Check-out time is any time in the next 24 hours. Just leave your keys on the bed."

At the cabins, they pulled the cars around and backed them in "just in case" they needed to leave in a hurry. They would rotate the watch schedule among the four of them to allow Tom to get some rest and hopefully unlock some more of his memory bank. The other agents would keep watch from the cabin across the way.

The next morning, they were awakened to the sound of automatic weapons fire coming from the front of the compound. Dr. Kafka sent one of the agents to investigate while the rest of the team stood ready to protect Tom. The agent came back and reported that there were three bodies between a car and the office. But everything seemed safe. Just then the Manager came walking up carrying some very serious. Looking artillery.

"Just checking on how you all are doing. It seems those three young fellows were not really being very polite and asked if you were here. When they started insulting my wife, it was time to teach them something about manners. Unfortunately for them, they were very slow learners."

"Most campground Managers really don't have the kind of armament you're carrying," observed Dr. Kafka.

"I was with a law enforcement agency that will remain unnamed for about 20 years. When I saw the type of weapons you all were trying to conceal when you checked in, so we took our standard precautions. Incidentally, young lady, looking at May, you are carrying so much metal that I was afraid you're going to set off the TSA alarms at the airport ten miles away. The type of armament you all are showing is usually available only to government agencies. So, I assumed y'all were here for something other than a corporate weekend. We let you be about your business until those gentlemen showed up, and I had to intervene."

"We're just passing through, but would you allow me to reimburse you for expenses you incurred on our behalf? Would an extra $20,000 be reasonable since bullets are so expensive nowadays?" asked Dr. Kafka.

"That sounds reasonable," said the Manager, "And since I know you're probably going to want to leave as soon as possible, the Mrs. prepared a little extra something so you won't starve to death until lunch."

At that point, Joan came up in a golf cart with three large plastic styrofoam ice chests loaded with foodstuffs and several gallons of her coffee.

"Now, here's a bit of breakfast since I know you all are going to be hungry, having to get up so early to leave."

She explained, "In that bag, there is some leftover pie just in case you want a little snack along the way."

"Joan," said Dr. Kafka, "you are so kind. If you ever get bored with life in a campground, I have a job waiting for you for the rest of your life. As for you, Mr. Manager, do you need any help attending to the garbage in front?"

"Not a problem. I've got a friend of mine coming over who deals with garbage, so you all just be on your way and be safe."

"Okay, the rest of you get the cars packed, and let's leave. "Here's the rest that I owe you," said Dr. Kafka reaching into one of their cars and opening a hidden compartment where he pulled out a wad of bills and handed them to the Manager.

"Many thanks, and if any more of those people come around, y'all were here for the night and left early in the morning before I got up, so I don't know which way you went," said Dan.

"If you ever have a problem, call this number," said Dr. Kafka, writing a phone number on a business card.

"You will receive any help I can provide." Dr. Kafka got into the car. May gave Elaine a big hug and thanks while detecting a large caliber automatic under Elaine's apron, undoubtedly for use in the kitchen. The rest of the team got into their cars, and off they went.

Chapter 19

At the front of the campground, the team turned back the way they had come.

"Wait a minute," said Tom. "Are we going in the wrong direction?"

"We'll drive down this way for a few miles, then cut back," said Dr. Kafka.

"Hopefully, in case anybody was watching and saw us, they would have us heading in the wrong direction."

"Don't you ever get tired of this kind of life?" said Tom.

Chuckling to himself, Dr. Kafka said, "Actually, this kind of life, as you put it, is pretty mundane. Wait until things get exciting."

Both Tom and May felt their mouths drop open, which invoked laughter from Dr. Kafka and Bill, the driver.

"On a scale of 1 to 10, with 10 being the most excitement one can bear, so far this is about a five or six," said Dr. Kafka.

"I can hardly wait for it to get more exciting," muttered Tom sarcastically, and turning to May, "Are you part of this?"

May, looking at Dr. Kafka, said, "I'm just a secretary. Speaking of that, does it mean that all this extra time is overtime?"

I'll have to see about that," said Dr. Kafka.

"I'm on a rather tight budget, and you are already overpaid as is. Plus, you know I'm not deducting any of the food and housing costs you are using….so far," with a twinkle in his eye.

They turned at the intersection that would connect them with a parallel road that headed in their original direction, hopefully having thrown off any pursuers. After several hours of travel and it seemed they were alone, they pulled off at a lovely little park to rest and explore the ice chests of foodstuffs provided by Joan.

"If this is how government people eat regularly, I'm all for government work," said Tom, waving a chicken fried drumstick to emphasize his statement.

"There are some advantages to having the boss buy lunch for us poor peons," said the driver between mouthfuls of a succulent roast beef sandwich on homemade bread.

"The major question of the day is how much pie will be left for the likes of us?" said May as she made a grab for the pie, but the driver was already protectively holding it.

The ensuing verbal repartee threatened to continue beyond everyone's lifetime until Dr. Kafka stated in a very authoritative voice, "Stop that, Children!"

"Doc, would you dissect the pie to ensure that we all get a fair share of the body," at which point all participants had a good laugh as the doctor produced a pair of gloves and proceeded to "dissect" the pie with almost inhuman precision that ensured everybody received an equal amount.

After the pie was consumed along with the last of the wonderful coffee, which had been kept steaming hot in some sort of high-tech thermos provided by Joan, Tom asked the question that was on everyone's mind.

"Where are we going?" "That depends on you," said Dr. Kafka.

"First, up ahead at Scottsdale, we're meeting with another team to reinforce us. Then it's up to you, Tom. I have the actual latitude from the hidden room at the Pentagon. Supposedly, you were given the longitude in your imprinting. We were supposed to put this together at the ranch, but all we can do now is hope that you will go deep enough into your mind to find the rest of the address without any of my high-tech support equipment."

"I was afraid you would ask me that," said Tom.

"I have been searching my mind to see if I have any idea where we are going. All I have been able to dredge up has been a picture of a goat on the side of a mountain," said Tom.

"When we pick up the other team, one of the members is an expert at computer research and might be able to help us."

"Well," said Tom, "my daughter-in-law does research for an oil company and probably could find the answer in about two minutes. Can we contact her?"

"No," said Dr. Kafka.

"You know that this is above top-secret, so don't even think about contacting her or anybody else. We don't know who's monitoring our radio/phone calls. The reason I think that we are being monitored is the ease at which the terrorists intercepted our phone calls to our travel desk. Either they are somehow monitoring our supposed secure communication, or there is a mole inside our organization. Either way, don't call anybody."

"Can I please call Mary and tell her I'm okay?"

"I said, don't call anybody!" exclaimed Dr. Kafka.

As they returned to their cars, May tapped Tom's arm and said, "I'm sure somebody will let her know you are okay."

"Still, I would feel much better telling her that myself," said Tom as they drove away.

Chapter 20

After five hours of intensive driving, with everybody constantly watching to see if they were being followed or were going to be attacked, they finally arrived at their destination, the Phoenician Resort in Scottsdale, Arizona.

"Wow," said May. "This is definitely out of the secretarial pay schedule."

"Ditto," said Tom. "Same for retired teachers."

"Double ditto for poor Mexican taxi drivers," said Bill, the driver (who was pulling in six figures a year for being a poor Mexican taxi driver).

"Now, hush. You all are here on business to meet the other team and to figure out the second half of our mission," said Dr. Kafka. "I'll check us in, and this time, let's leave most of our weapons in the car so we don't get a visit from the local gendarmes."

"At least can I keep a few things," said May. "Just maybe a gun and a knife?"

"Only if they don't show," said Dr. Kafka. "I'll go in and get our rooms while you all stay out here and try not to scare the guests. We look suspicious enough without any luggage. I'll tell the desk that when we got to Sky Harbor International Airport here in Phoenix, all our luggage made it to Honolulu."

When Dr. Kafka returned, he handed out the room keys and said that the other team was already there and was in the suite right across from theirs. "Also, there is a clothing shop downstairs in one of the corridors with an open account in the name of Thomas Investment Corporation. Get what you need for one complete set of clothing so that you can blend in with the rest of the guests. The rest of your clothing and equipment we'll get in town."

The team dutifully went up to their rooms, which turned out to be multiple suites. After a long hot shower, each team member went down to the clothing store. There, they were forced to get clothing that was commonly found on Rodeo Drive in Hollywood, California. Tom's slacks, sports shirt, shoes, socks and underwear came to more than he made in several months as a teacher. He also took advantage of getting a haircut and shaving at the barbershop, i.e., Stylist Salon.

May got a pants outfit and shoes and availed herself of the spa services. She also sneaked in a lightweight summer dress just in case she had to go somewhere. Bill, the driver, while outfitting himself with designer blue jeans and a Western-style silk shirt, kept complaining that he could feed his family for a month on what his shirt cost. But the job forced him to have to fit in, so he had to suffer in order to blend in with the group.

Dr. K came out looking like a multimillionaire (which he was). He also availed himself of a haircut, beard trim, and manicure, all of which seemed as if this was a regular vacation for him. May became a little suspicious when the staff seemed to know Dr. Kafka by his first name, almost as if he had been there before. When they all retired to the main suite, Dr. Kafka called the other team to come over. When they walked in, Tom's jaw dropped so low that the doctor thought he was going to have to put it in a sling to get it back to normal.

"Mary!" exclaimed Tom. "What are you doing here?"

And then as the other two members of the team walked in, Tom could only gasp.

"Corky and Elaine! What are you all doing here?" he said, almost collapsing as Mary ran over and gave him a huge hug.

"We are the other team," said Mary.

"Corky and Elaine have been with the agency for a few years and, I might add," said Dr. Kafka, "they are one of our most effective teams because who would suspect a young husband-and-wife on honeymoon courtesy of a rich uncle sending them to exotic places in the world?"

"But Mary," asked Tom, "why are you here?"

"Silly boy. I have been your bodyguard all these years. Remember all those women's retreats that I would go to two or three times a year? Those were to requalify certain weapons and techniques. Along the way, I fell in love with you." May broke in with a big smile and said, "I can see why. He's a keeper."

"May, I want to thank you for keeping him safe all this time. If it had been anybody else, I would never have agreed to this arrangement. Especially since it was my son Corky whom you beat in the final test," said Mary with a twinkle in her eye, at which point Corky chimed in.

"I still get headaches when it rains, thanks to you. But in a rematch, you will not be so lucky," Corky said laughingly.

"The details of your family reunion can wait until later," said Dr. Kafka. "Elaine, Tom says he can remember an image of a goat on the side of a mountain. Here is the longitude line that we have from the Pentagon attack. Can you find the place?"

"With all the attention that we have been getting lately, I think we are under a time constraint. If it can be found, I will find it," said Elaine. "Where do you want me to work?"

"How about right here since Tom's bedroom is over there," said Dr. Kafka, pointing to a bedroom that was almost a suite by itself. "If Mary doesn't mind, I'd like for you to take over from May to give her a rest."

"If May doesn't mind, I'll be glad to take over, although I don't think Tom will be getting much rest over the next day or so," said Mary with a sparkle in her eyes.

"I understand that room service is pretty good here, so I will have to stay in my bedroom where Mary can keep an eye on me. And I need to be on call in case Mary needs me," said Tom.

"I'm sure something can be arranged to be mutually satisfactory to all parties concerned," replied Dr. Kafka.

"I will need Corky around to protect me and act as a gopher. So, Corky, order up something while I get my gear set up," said Elaine.

"Now I can see who rules the roost in our family," quipped Tom. "You must have gotten some tips from Mary because I recognize the similarities."

"No, as you know, my family was military, and a lot of times, I had to take charge of my three brothers, who are a bit older but had the good sense not to argue with me," quipped Elaine as she turned and headed out the door across the hall to get her computer stuff.

Chapter 21

Elaine returned to the main suite carrying what appeared to be a military-type armored computer.

"Boy, that looks like a serious computer," said May, looking enviously at the device. "What does it have inside?"

"Well, since you ask, it has an Intel Xeon E5 – 2679 V for a CPU with 10 terabytes of storage. It also has the capability of satellite transmission and reception, plus the touch screen is virtually indestructible. On top of that, it makes a great milkshake. Just joking," said Elaine. "The battery life is good for three hours of continuous use. However, you have to be careful where it is sitting because it can get very hot, and I mean very hot. Another plus is that the top of the unit is also a very effective solar charger and can recharge the whole thing in about four hours of direct sunlight."

"Now you got me drooling," said May. "What do I have to do to get one, promise my firstborn to the government?"

"Almost," said Elaine. "I had to sign a ream of paperwork and have the computer synced to my eyes and fingerprint."

"Why so heavy on the biometrics?" Asked Mary.

"The way it is set is that if someone were to try to use it without the proper biometrics, the system would self-destruct with a small EMP bursting and a small explosion. And seriously, I do mean explosion," said Elaine.

"In that case, why don't you set up in one of the bedrooms just in case something goes wrong," said Tom.

"Oh, it's perfectly safe," smiled Elaine, "as long as no one fools with it. Besides, the replacement cost is worth $20,000, and if we lost it, it could be remotely destroyed, but then Corky and I would have the cost deducted from our paychecks or hides or both," said Elaine.

"What!" exclaimed Corky.

"Well, dear, you were so busy playing with your toys and shooting up the target range so badly that when we were asked to leave, you didn't hear me explain the parameters of having it assigned to us," quipped Elaine as she headed towards one of the bedrooms to set up and begin her search.

"How long will we be here?" Asked Tom.

"Actually, that depends a lot on you and Elaine to tell us where to go next. I can give Elaine a latitude starting point that showed up in the safe at the Pentagon, but the longitude will have to be worked out between you and Elaine. Somewhere around latitude 19.5 N. is a mountain with an Image of a goat on it, according to you. Tom, If you can remember anything else that will help Elaine locate her objective, please feel free to chime in," said Dr. Kafka. "That's why I want you to stay up here with May and Corky acting as guards. I'm going into town with Bill to get some necessities. The Doc and Jim will remain across the hall. Any room service that you request will be delivered over there, just in case. Doc can test it before bringing it over. Any questions?" Asked Dr. Kafka.

"Well," said Tom, "It's going to be rough to have to stay with my wife and suffer gourmet room service in these palatial suites, but I think I can do it."

"You darn well better," exclaimed Mary, slapping him on the back of his head. "You survived 30 years with considerably less, so get used to it," she said with a big smile on her face."

"Any other questions?" said Dr. Kafka. "No, then I'll see you in a while," and he walked out the door.

"Well," said Mary, "since we have to suffer under these working conditions, I work best with a full stomach."

"I'm with you," said May.

"Well, since you all are being so insistent, I guess Corky and I should join you," said Elaine. "What about you, Tom?"

"I'll go with the flow," Tom replied.

After the team had placed their orders, which amounted to enough food for a small army and barely met the doctor's approval as being healthy, Elaine and May tried to help Tom recover any more information that could narrow down the search.

"That's all I can remember, but it's pretty clear what the goat looks like if I ever see it for real," said Tom.

"That's okay," said Elaine. "We will find it. We've got a rough idea on the latitude, and it sounds like it's gonna be somewhere in the southwest, so I'll start looking there."

Before Elaine could start her search, the phone rang. It was Doc saying that the food passed his test, and he was ready to send it over. May went over to the door and opened it as Doc rolled in several carts, groaning under the weight of food. "You sure this is enough?" he said.

"Don't worry. We'll try to survive with this," said May, snagging several bacon strips as the carts passed by.

Why me?

During lunch/breakfast, Tom caught up with the other side of his family's activities. He learned that Corky, while in college studying to be a geologist, was also in the Army ROTC. "I thought that was just a fad," said Tom. "Since you didn't mention it very much, I assumed you dropped out."

"Not quite. It seems the army was very interested in my geology expertise, and I could meet the physical requirements for Ranger school. So, after graduation, I wound up working with Army intelligence under the cover of working for an oil company," Elaine said. "And, as you know, I was working on completing an advanced degree in computer science. I also happened to be in ROTC, where I told you I met Corky and was also able to complete the same physical training as Corky. It turned out that since we were getting married, the Army figured out they might as well put us out as a team with Army intelligence. It turned out that we were a little too successful at what we were doing and needed to lay low for a while. That's when Dr. Kafka recruited us for the duration. But first, we had to pass the same series of tests that May did to get the job."

"You two had to pass the same tests I did," said May with an incredulous look on her face.

"Yes, and before he starts bragging about how he beat my time in the Maze, it was because the guy I had to drag to the box must have weighed 300 pounds, and it took me a while to get him there. That's the only reason Corky beat me," said Elaine.

Tom looked at Mary and asked, "What was your part in all of this?"

"Well, at first, I was assigned to you based on your psychological profile. My job's function was the same as May's: to be your bodyguard. But after about five minutes, I knew I was going to become more than just a bodyguard. I fell in love with you," said Mary, reaching out across the table and resting her hand on Tom's.

"It took you that long?" exclaimed May.

"Hush, dear, he's mine," smiled Mary. "The hard part was finding time between watching out for him, taking care of the kids, keeping current with my training, and trying to find places to store weapons without a set of very nosy kids finding them. Tom, why do you think I was so much in agreement with your putting in a workshop? Why do you think the bank agreed so readily for the funding it provided, that we use their recommended contractor, and that the work could be done while you are away for a summer institute? I guess it's okay to tell you now that your workshop has a basement where I keep my toys below, and you keep your stuff upstairs. It worked out very well over the years, didn't it, Love?"

"For all these years, I don't understand how you and the kids were able to do what you were doing right under my nose without my noticing," said Tom.

"You did, Dear, but you are easily distracted physically, like the time you asked me about a bruise on my backside, and I took you into the bedroom and demonstrated where I could've gotten it from," said Mary.

"I don't think we need to go any further, Mom," said Corky. "I'll have a mental picture that I won't be able to get rid of for the rest of my life."

"I don't know about that. I remember once when we were…" Mary continued.

"Enough," said Corky, whose face was starting to turn slightly red.

"We have work to do, and sitting around enjoying and telling stories aren't going to get it done. I always think my family's history is fascinating. Still, you two go ahead and get back to work in your room, and I'll make sure the leftovers don't go to waste," May said while spooning another mouthful of banana foster into her mouth.

Chapter 22

While the crew spent the remainder of the day resting, Dr. Kafka and Bill drove over to Sky Harbor International Airport, where they boarded a small, unmarked Learjet. The jet took off and headed west toward Los Angeles. On board, Dr. Kafka made three secure encrypted phone calls. Two calls were made to Washington D., C. And one call was made to Los Angeles. One of the calls to Washington was to provide a progress report to the White House, and the other call went to a somewhat non-descript office building down the street from the White House. The Los Angeles call was to request a meeting with "resources" at the Ontario airport.

"Well, Bill," said Dr. Kafka, "the fate of the world now depends on the 65-year-old brain of a retired schoolteacher to somehow recover a potential secret greater than that of the development of the atomic bomb. What do you think our chances are?"

"If I were a betting man, Boss, and you know I am not," said the man who was on a first-name basis in most of the major racetracks' high roller suites around the country, "I would say our chances are better placed on betting when the next tsunami will hit Denver, Colorado."

"I'll drink to that," laughed Dr. Kafka.

Dr. K's plane landed at Ontario International Airport in Ontario, California, instead of Los Angeles International Airport. As they were on final approach, Bill pointed out the window and said, "Why is that 747 parked at the general aviation side and not at the main terminal?"

Dr. Kafka replied, "That's the reason why we are here."

"Who or what is on it?" asked Bill.

"We're about to find out," said Dr. Kafka as his plane taxied up to the general aviation reception area. As they deplaned, they were met by a young woman holding up a sign with Dr. K on it.

Since there was nobody else in the reception area, Bill said, "I guess that's for you." Just as the young woman approached them, asking if one of them was Dr. Kafka.

"That must be me," replied Dr. Kafka.

"May I see some identification?" said the young woman.

Dr. Kafka presented his photo ID, which she scrutinized very carefully.

"Now," said Bill, "let's look at your identification."

"I am the Chief of Staff of the VP, and here is my ID," she said, looking pointedly at Bill, who produced his ID and said, "I'm Dr. Kafka's driver, gofer, whatever."

"You are also a world-class gambler, world-class driver, and a multimillionaire in your right," said the woman.

"You must have me mixed up with somebody else. I'm just a Mexican taxi driver," muttered Bill in his best broken Spanish.

"Right, and the Cubs will win the pennant this year," said the woman with a twinkle in her eye. Gentlemen, if you will please follow me, the Vice President is waiting."

Chapter 23

As they walked across a short distance from the reception area to the 747, Bill couldn't help but notice there were no markings on the plane.

"That's right," said the woman. "We aren't here. This is just a standby charter plane in case there's a problem at LAX. At least that's what everybody is being told," she said as they walked up the boarding stairs.

"So that's why you are wearing the kind of stewardess uniform, to throw off any curious people," observed Bill.

"Actually, this is my uniform. In my younger days, I was a real stewardess. That's how I got through college," she said as she escorted them through the door into the interior of a plane that was fitted out in a luxurious corporate setting with three very big, very serious Secret Service agents who then went through the ID routine again with Dr. Kafka and Bill.

They were finally led down a short hall to a conference room where the Vice President, the Hon. Henry Madison, was seated. Dr. Kafka was invited in, and Bill wasn't. Bill was escorted past the conference room to a small dining room at the rear of the plane.

"Are you hungry?" asked the woman. "The VP usually keeps his meetings short, but I can whip up a sandwich or something if you'd like?" "Well, what are you offering?" said Bill.

"According to your dossier, you prefer roast beef on rye with horseradish and mustard, Swiss cheese, and a little lettuce."

"Sounds great. Is there anything else in my dossier that I should know about?" "Anyone who works for Dr. Kafka gets that back to their birth. Yours was normal. After 12 ½ hours, your mother said you came out screaming and haven't stopped talking since," said the woman with a grin while she deftly assembled the sandwich with a skill that indicated some culinary training.

"Since you're still working, I can offer soda, iced tea, or water."

"Then I'll have Long Island iced tea," replied Bill.

"Listen, Smart Ass, I said iced tea, no alcohol," replied the woman. She then served him what was, in his eyes, a perfect sandwich.

"Who am I to argue with a beautiful senorita, especially one who has a large automatic tucked where she thinks it doesn't show? But with your perfect body, any blemish such as a gun stands out like a sore thumb," replied Bill, laughing.

"Would you care to join me?" "I'll just have a glass of iced tea and make sure you eat everything just like I have to do with my kids," she said, pouring herself a glass of iced tea while secretly laughing at Bill's sudden uncomfortable look and ensuing silence.

"Come on in and sit down," said the VP. "You want something to drink?"

"No thanks," said Dr. Kafka.

"Then let's get right to it. What has your team accomplished so far?"

"We are positioned to make the final jump as soon as Tom narrows down the location of Site Alpha. Our cover appears to be intact, but we may need to have additional backup once we get there."

"The best I can do is to provide a detachment of local National Guard, but the President wants to keep the attention on your project as low as possible."

Why me?

"Do you have any additional information for me on Site Apache?"

"All I know is that our other site has been unable to identify all of the components in this sample piece of metal that was found in the safe at the Pentagon," said the VP, handing Dr. Kafka a piece of metal about the size of his palm.

"It's very light," observed Dr. Kafka. "Our scientists at the Livermore labs have been unable to bend it, cut it, or do anything else to it, plus it's anti-magnetic," said the VP.

"In all my 85 years, I've never encountered anything like it," said Dr. Kafka. "Just off the top of my head, if we can reproduce this material, it will revolutionize almost every area of technology that we know about today."

"I hope that now you have some inkling beyond just obtaining the location of Site Apache. Those in the know feel that the site may just be the greatest national treasure that we have. That's why it's critical you all get to it first and hold it," said the Vice President, retrieving the piece of material from Dr. Kafka.

"Get back to your team and appoint two others along with yourself to keep me updated, okay? The reason is that you survived three wars and, just in case your time runs out, the mission must continue," said the Vice President.

At that point, he pressed a buzzer on the phone, and when the young woman came in, he said, "Please escort these two men back to their plane."

Turning to Dr. Kafka, he said, "The only thing I can say is Godspeed and good luck," he shook his hand, and then the young lady escorted Dr. Kafka out the door. On the way back to their plane, the woman gave Dr. Kafka a small lunch cooler, saying, "Since you didn't get a chance to eat, I've included a small salad and pastrami sandwich on rye for you. And I included an extra sandwich for this bottomless pit walking beside you."

"That's a very astute observation," said Dr. Kafka.

"Now you know why we don't let him order à la carte whenever we eat out. Otherwise, the hit on the national debt would be astounding."

"I'm just a growing boy," said the 36-year-old driver, "but if that sandwich is as good as the one she made on the plane, it won't last for the walk over to our plane, now that I know what's in there."

Reaching for the cooler, his hand was stopped by a young, incredibly strong but delicate-looking hand. "No, you don't. You can wait until you're on board the plane. And, Dr. Kafka, just so you know, there are two pieces of coconut cream pie for your desserts. One for you and one for what's his name."

"Thank you. I will see that this cooler does not get opened until we are at cruising altitude," said Dr. Kafka.

"But I'll starve to death," exclaimed Bill.

"Then we will drop your body off somewhere over the ocean," said Dr. Kafka, eliciting a laugh from the woman.

"You know, for a taxi driver, he sure has a mouth on him, so I may have to eat his pie just to teach him a lesson about manners."

To that remark, Bill muttered, "I'll be good, so let's get the plane off the ground so we can eat. If she wasn't married, I would marry her today just for her cooking."

"Who said I was married? I said I watched children, which is what I do on my days off at the orphanage." With that, she gave Bill a wink, shook hands with Dr. Kafka, and closed the door to their plane.

Dr. Kafka's plane took off just ahead of the VP's 747, with Bill eyeing the cooler the whole time until they reached cruising altitude. When Dr. Kafka opened the cooler, he found a very small note addressed to Bill. He handed it to Bill, who read it with his eyes almost bugging out. What it said was, "Look me up when you're in Washington. My number is 387-876-2843. I'll show you what else I'm good at besides cooking. PS: I'm betting on FSU to win the title this year." Signed Diane Roberts.

Chapter 24

At the resort, Tom, Mary, and the kids began catching up. "I can't believe this is the family I thought I knew," exclaimed Tom.

"I thought we were the average American family. Instead, it turns out we are anything but."

"Darling, just calm down," said Mary affectionately, patting his arm. "We are an average family, but we all have a little something extra to our jobs that we just forgot to tell you about," said Mary.

"And, Dad," said Corky, "we do have the jobs we told you about, but the job description may have included a little more than usual. We are still the same family you have known for the last 30+ years."

"I can't believe I didn't catch on."

"Dear," said Mary, "you were too busy being a father, husband, teacher, and a pretty good lover."

"Mom," groaned both kids. "Are we supposed to be working," interjected Tom, trying to head off a potential discussion of his sex life.

"Elaine, how are you doing? Anything pop up yet?" "So far, I have five or six places, but I am trying to narrow them down some more. If I had more information, I could improve my search algorithm. Corky, why don't you and May relieve the crew across the way so they can get some clothes and relax a little?"

"I'm going to rest these old original bones for a bit," said Tom. "I'll tuck you in," said Mary, escorting Tom to the bedroom.

"Mary," said Tom, "last time you tucked me in, it took me two days to recover."

"Mom, Dad, please," groaned the kids. "Why can't you just nap like old folks are supposed to do, please."

"It's not quite nap time, but we will just talk or something until it's time," said Mary with a twinkle in her eye as she closed the door to the master suite. Then she grabbed Tom and gave him the biggest, longest kiss he could ever remember. When she finally stopped long enough for a breath, she whispered in his ear, "I wanted so long to tell you the rest of my story, and now I feel like a new woman with no secrets."

Tom suddenly jumped back and looked at Mary with a puzzled look in his eyes.

"What's wrong," said Mary. "Are you okay?" Tom muttered something, grabbed the door, and stumbled out into the living room.

"Well, that didn't take long, must be old age," quipped Corky. Joan said, looking at Corky, "I've heard someone is known as Flash, but I can't remember who they were talking about. Can you help me, Brother?"

"Children, enough," chided Mary. "Your father is having an attack of some sort. Corky, get the doctor."

As Corky turned toward the door, Tom stammered,

"Wait. I'm okay, but I just had a data dump, and I think I know the location of something."

"At least sit down and tell us," said Mary. Tom dropped on the couch, took a deep breath, and said, "All I have is a bunch of letters, numbers, and a name. Does Moab mean anything?"

"What country is that?" asked Corky.

"You know better than that, Child," said Joan. "It is a town somewhere in Utah. I think that's near one of the mountains I have been able to identify. Let me check," said Joan, rapidly clicking some keys on her computer.

"Here it is," she said. "It's on the right longitude and latitude. Let's tell Dr. Kafka and see what he wants to do."

"Okay, but after that, I need some rest." Tom stumbled into the bedroom and literally fell into the bed asleep before his body contacted the bed.

"Mom," said Joan, "you've got to teach me how you did that." "Child, don't you have work to do?" said Mary, her face showing just a tinge of red.

"Yes, Ma'am," said Joan. "But later… Hush," said Mary with a sparkle in her eye, promising a very interesting mother/daughter conversation when time permitted.

Chapter 25

Dr. Kafka and Bill's plane landed on the commercial side of the Phoenix airport. No one noticed the small commuter plane parked on the tarmac among the other private and corporate aircraft. But the commuter plane's pilot, who was sitting in the lounge waiting for orders, did notice Bill from before as the taxi driver who frequented the area of the hacienda. He quickly dialed the number on one of the burner phones given to him by the leader to relate this possible observation.

The reply was short and direct. "Follow him," and then there was a click as the other party hung up. The pilot cracked the phone, took out the Sim card, and dropped various parts of the phone are in different trash cans inside and outside the terminal. Outside, he saw Bill and Dr. Kafka waiting as the next taxi in line pulled up. The pilot waited until the next taxi pulled up, got in, and told the driver to follow the other taxi. He said that they were staying at the same place but forgot and was too embarrassed to ask where so he could follow them.

"I can call the dispatcher for you and ask where he's going if you would like?" said the driver.

"Please do," said the pilot. "But please don't tell them why because I will never hear the end of it at the office," said the pilot, pressing a $20 bill through the money slot by the driver.

"Will do," said the driver, picking up the money and his cell phone instead of the cab's radio mike. After the call, the driver said, "They're heading to the Phoenician." "That's the place, now I remember, thanks," said the pilot.

The pilot pulled up just in time to see Bill and Dr. Kafka walking through the front doors.

"Thanks, keep the change," said the pilot, tossing twice the indicated fair into the till and getting out of the taxi. As he hurried through the door into the lobby, he saw Bill and Dr. Kafka getting into the elevator. The light stopped at the top floor and then the elevator came back down empty. The pilot used his last burner phone and called a different number.

When it was answered, he said, "They are on the top floor of the West Wing of the hotel."

"Wait, we will be there in six hours," was the reply. What the pilot didn't know was that it was standard operating procedure to go up in one wing and take the cross over to the other wing and down one floor. The pilot went to the reservation desk and asked to book a room on the top floor of the West Wing.

"I'm sorry," said the clerk. "That whole wing is booked up for a week."

"Is there any other floor available? "Well, the second floor from the top in the East Wing was just booked last night for at least one week, but I do have a suite on that top floor that's available."

The pilot appeared to think for a minute and then said, "I'll take it for three nights; how much?"

"That's $1800 per night," said the clerk and, looking at the pilot's clothes, added, "There is a 10% deposit of $600. What credit card do you want to use?" The pilot handed the clerk a platinum American Express card from a special fund in a national bank that allowed the card to be cleared in minimum time. The clerk gave him his card key and asked if he had any baggage.

"Yes, but it was supposed to be here, so I need to have my office track it down. I'll just go up and take a bath and rest. It's been a long trip."

"Very well," said the clerk. As soon as he got on the elevator, the pilot stopped at the 23rd floor and stuck his head out to check the hallway. All he saw was an empty breakfast cart outside of room 2304. The pilot carefully noted that number and then pressed 24 for the next floor to head up to where his suite was located.

In his room, the pilot, who had a degree in engineering, sat at the desk in his suite, waiting for the rest of the terrorist team to arrive. He was awakened from a brief sleep of exhaustion by the burner phone in his pocket.

"We will not be there until morning. We are having to bring in our remaining comrades, and they have encountered travel problems."

"How many do you have?" asked the pilot. "Eleven, counting myself."

"That's not enough." "With Allah it is," was the reply, and then the phone clicked off.

"With these people, I'm not sure that it's going to be enough for us. We will need the element of surprise. I have floors in two different towers. How can I narrow it down because once we start searching, we will probably lose all element of surprise."

Why me?

Then his head dropped down again, and he fell into an exhaustive sleep from almost 3 days of being awake searching for these infidels. The pilot woke up almost 4 hours later with his head resting against the top of the desk. As he raised his head, he saw the writing on the phone.

"To call another room, dial pound and then room number."

"That's it! How simple, Allah be praised. Rather than going down each hallway and knocking on each door, I can call each room and see who answers."

He pulled out the little notepad these Americans were so fond of putting in rooms and began to write down the suite numbers on each floor. He dialed each suite on the West Wing. All five suites answered with background music, laughing and squealing.

"Must be a hell of a party," he thought. Then he dialed the five suites on the floor below him in the East Wing. Only two answered and three went to voicemails. He remembered seeing the empty food cart and decided they would have to attack both rooms tomorrow. If the infidels were not there, then the team would try the West Wing. He ordered room service to feed his stomach, which had little in it the last several days. In the midst of his planning possible escape routes, room service arrived with a meal that any sultan would welcome. After eating, the pilot showered and fell asleep naked in bed, thinking about tomorrow.

Chapter 26

After landing, Dr. Kafka and Bill returned to the resort. There, they found the team in a happy mood.

"It's in Moab, Utah," said Joan, "or at least I think it is. Tom remembered a little more that helped to pin down our choices."

"It must have been Mom's tucking him in that did it," quipped Corky, at which a round of laughter erupted from the group.

Then Dr. Kafka, knowing a double meaning when he heard one, said, "If tucking him in were so helpful, maybe you should be tucking him in more," at which the room again was treated to another round of hilarious laughter.

"If what you say is right, we will need transportation and appropriate equipment. Bill, you work with Joan, Corky, and May to decide on an equipment list," said Dr. K.

The team went to work with Bill and John, an agent with a logistics background, figuring out distances and time. They decided on Range Rovers or trucks with crew cabs and began calling various car dealers in town looking for used vehicles.

When they found the right combination of car and truck, Dr. Kafka handed them a credit card and said, "Use this one and tell the auto people that we will need all-terrain tires. We will pay a bonus if we can pick them up today," said Dr. Kafka.

Corky said, "That is all rocky desert and mountains, so we will have a list of equipment based on that info. We will need boots for everybody, but anybody who has worn boots knows you must try them on for a fit."

"No, you don't," said Dr. Kafka. "Just get everyone's size and buy that plus the next size on each side. If the fit is too loose, you just put on more socks."

"Yes, Sir," said May. Here's a credit card. Try not to buy too much at any place to keep the curiosity factor down."

"Yes, Sir," said Corky. "Come on, May, we have a week's worth of shopping in a few hours."

"Don't forget the doctor and the agents across the hall," said Dr. Kafka. "On it," said May, pulling out a notepad and getting shoes and clothing sizes from everybody while Corky went across the room to do the same.

Chapter 27

After a Herculean effort, everything was attended to. The car dealership moved with a speed directly proportional to the size of the promised bonuses. This was good because Corky needed the truck to haul 30+ pairs of boots and camping equipment, and one of the Suburbans that the team arrived in to haul the remaining clothing, packs, and miscellaneous equipment to the resort. Getting all those supplies to the suite presented a challenge Dr. Kafka solved by telling the maître d' he was having a huge family party and needed to sneak the presents up to one of the suites he had on their floor. The five $100 bills ensured complete cooperation and the use of a service elevator. The clothing and shoes all made it up without a hitch. Everybody took turns entering the "Christmas room" to pick out and pack their "presents."

Dr. Kafka went last and found that May and Bill didn't believe his size, so they got a special trunk filled with secondhand mismatched clothing and shoes. When Dr. Kafka opened the trunk, he exploded. They almost had to call the doctor to calm him down. But after they all had a good laugh, May and Bill pulled out a suitcase filled with appropriate clothing.

After he packed, Dr. Kafka said, "Take your stuff down and pack the Range Rover." When everybody was back, they reviewed the plans for the next day. We will leave at 7 a.m., so get a good night's sleep. If you are going to 'tuck Tom in,' do it early so he can get a good night's rest. At that point, Mary blushed appropriately while the others laughed. The same goes for you, Bill. I want you to rest up well."

"But, Boss, you know how I must work out before sleeping just to get rested properly."

"Be in by 12," was the reply. Bill looked forlorn, hung his head, and said, "Yes, Boss." Again, a round of laughter ensued.

"See you in the morning," said Dr. Kafka as he walked out the door to spend a quiet night with a good cognac, make phone calls to update those who needed to know, and get some backup support commitments, if necessary.

Chapter 28

The next morning, the group had a room service breakfast that required five hotel waiters to deliver five food carts loaded to the max with the kinds of meals that can only be provided by a five-star resort. A sixth cart was filled with various containers containing liquids at the appropriate temperature.

As the team attacked the various foodstuffs, Dr. K remarked, "For people who are supposedly watching their diets, you sure are piling it on."

"There are two factors that allow us to do it like this. One: We checked with you, and you didn't say we shouldn't. (Of course, asking his permission while he was in the shower may have had something to do with his not saying anything.) The second reason is it's a known fact that the more expensive food is, the healthier it is for you. And you want us to be as healthy as possible… right?" quipped Mary. At which, Dr. K almost choked on his Aruba dark coffee, knowing he was the one who would have to justify this bill to the bean counters in Washington.

"In that case," replied Dr. Kafka, "you all will be healthy for at least four or five days."

"You mean four or five hours," replied Bill, which elicited a glare from Dr. Kafka while the group broke into a needed round of laughter.

After eating, the group made one last bathroom stop and sanitized the room to ensure there was no information about what they would be doing next. Before they left, Dr. K requested early room cleaning, so the room service crew moved in just as they were leaving by one of the other service elevators and stairs.

Once downstairs, they moved quickly to the vehicles, started them, and left. Barely two minutes later, three service vans pulled up to the delivery entrance, and all 15 workers began unloading laundry carts and headed up the same service elevator to the ninth floor, where they armed themselves with weapons hidden inside their carts. When they rushed into the suites, they only found several of the room service workers who had to change uniforms and underwear later. The leader questioned the staff and found out the occupants had just left. The terrorists then rushed to the elevator and burst out onto an empty parking lot. They were able to elicit a description of the vehicles from the attendant who said he heard talk about something in Utah. He was strangled and placed on his chair in the parking lot kiosk. The attendant wasn't discovered for 20 minutes and only when a tourist tried to ask for directions. The screams were loud enough to cause hotel security to activate without having to be called.

The group took the 17 north towards Flagstaff, where they had a leisurely lunch at the Golden Arches. (Dr. K said they blew the food budget on breakfast.) Then, on to the 89 to the 160, where they camped at the San Juan River just off the 160 because of early darkness. The campsite was very primitive by Dr. K's standards. There wasn't any room service or gourmet food, but it did have running water, was secluded, and had room for all their cars and tents. Cooking used some food that Mary bought at various stores, insisting that they may need to camp out. This idea of camping food included steaks, wine, and fresh vegetables. Fortunately, many group had camping experience and could table a decent meal. After the meal, a rotating watch was set up with staggered intervals to throw off any pattern someone could use. Several of the group, mostly younger people, started a campfire "to act like a corporate holiday group."

It was a relief to get away from the last few days of "drama" and just be themselves for at least a short while. And while it was not cold, there was a tendency for several people to sit closer together "for warmth." Of course, those not campers let it be known that sleeping on the ground was not to their liking, and then the next morning they complained that scrambled eggs, bacon, fruit, and coffee were a very limited breakfast. However, Dr. K was observed eating more and complaining less as he discovered that Mary and Wayne were excellent camp cooks.

When Cara quizzed Mary about her training, Mary just smiled and said, "Feeding Cub Scouts, Brownies, Boy Scouts, Girl Scouts, and soccer teams teaches one a lot about using simple foods to feed an army." She admitted to writing a Dutch oven cookbook and teaching Dutch oven cooking for many years as a scout leader.

Since this was the first time the group could test out the camping equipment that Corky and Elaine bought, they found that putting sleeping bags back into their stuff bags wasn't as easy as taking them out the first time. Testing out their boots became a priority, and they had to scuff them up a bit and add some dust on them so they would not look brand-new to the outdoors. Around noon, after another great camping meal of chicken and rice, cornbread, and iced tea, finished with a dump cake cooked in the Dutch ovens that Mary insisted they purchase as part of the camping supplies, they packed up and left. Tom remarked to Dr. Kafka that he had Cub Scouts who could pack faster and neater with less groaning than this group. It seems that Dr. K was mistakenly waiting for someone to pack for him. After another round of laughter, they left and turned back on the 160N. They took the precaution of allowing other vehicles to pass before pulling onto the road to prevent looking like a convoy. They turned off onto the 119 to Moab.

Chapter 29

"We missed them," reported the team leader to Mohammed, who seemed to explode and shout into the radio.

"Get downstairs and find someone who knows where they went. We will search all the suites to see if we can find out anything." Fifteen minutes later, the team leader called and said, "The parking lot attendant said he heard them talking about Utah, and they left in three cars and a truck. Since he no longer had anything to say, we encouraged his silence."

Mohammed thought for a moment, then ordered the pilot to get into the air and check the main road to Utah. "On my way," came the reply from the pilot, who then took the elevator down to the front desk, where he asked for his bill. While paying, he casually asked what the best way was to visit some of the parks advertised on the brochure he picked up by the elevator.

The clerk said, "The fastest way is to take the 17 to Salt Lake City and get specific directions from there. It just so happens that we have a wonderful facility there, and I would be glad to make reservations for you."

"No thanks," said the pilot. "I like to discover things on my own at different places and adventures." Upon leaving, he caught a shuttle in front of the resort to the airport rather than taking a taxi, so no record would be made of his leaving the resort. The rest of the terrorists returned to their trucks and pulled out past the dead attendant. Further down the road they pulled into a motel on the outskirts of Scottsdale to wait on additional information from the pilot or other sources.

The pilot obtained a map from a car rental agency at the airport. He took off under a VFR (visual flight rules) flight plan, which allowed him to fly pretty freely over the area. He picked up the 17N and followed it north all the way to Salt Lake City, not seeing anything that looked like a group of three cars and a truck. He refueled at Salt Lake Airport and retraced his flight path. Since it was getting dark when he got to Scottsdale, he landed and called the leader to inform him he hadn't seen any group of three cars and a truck on the main road into Salt Lake. The leader said tomorrow at first light check each turnoff for a half hour or less. "I will have two of our group meet you at the airport at 0500 hrs., ready to leave with you at first light."

"I'll meet them at 0500 hrs. at the general aviation reception area," said the pilot, who then hung up, destroyed the burner phone he used, and caught a shuttle ride to a nearby motel to rest and get a bit to eat.

The next morning, the pilot got to the airport at 0430 hrs., but the two members were already there waiting. The man and woman both looked like they needed some sleep. The woman said they hadn't rested since they got to Scottsdale. When the pilot expressed his concern, the man said, "Allah provides what we need." While the pilot pretended to work on a flight plan, he showed the couple how to use another Western decadent device called a vending machine and bought each of them a cup of strong black coffee and something called a coffee cake. After a quick coffee, snack, and bathroom trip, the trio walked out to the plane, ran the checklist, then taxied out to the active runway and took off.

Chapter 30

Once in the air, the trio began searching each road with an off-ramp between the Utah border and Salt Lake City. Every three hours, they had to land for fuel, coffee, and a bathroom. After almost 12 hours of searching, the pilot reported back that they hadn't seen any convoy of three cars and a truck. And there wasn't much traffic on the road, so it was easy to check out vehicles. They did see several groups of two vehicles, usually a car and a tractor-trailer truck, all spaced out almost the same distance from each other along the 119. But due to needing to refuel, they didn't find them again. "Okay," said Mohammad, "I'll send two teams along the 119 and one team along the 17 to Salt Lake City. I'm still waiting for our brothers to see if they can get anything from the data dump we sent them from our raid on the ranch. Pilot, are there any towns along 119 with an airport where I can meet you?"

"The nearest one of any note is at a place called Moab. I flew over it, and the town is very isolated but appears large, and the airport has a tower."

"Good, I'll meet you there and wait for something from either our brothers at home or Allah to guide us further."

"See you at the airport reception area at 900 hours tomorrow," replied the pilot, who then turned his plane northeast towards Moab.

Chapter 31

The team enjoyed the beautiful, rugged scenery for the rest of the long, uneventful trip to Moab. There, they found two motels next to each other. The men got rooms, saying they were engineers for the gas company here to learn about how to operate a gas distribute system. The women posing as wives got their own rooms as did those posing as secretaries to the big boss, Dr. Kafka..

After settling in and eating at separate tables across the street at a diner, they established a watch schedule. Tom, Mary, Corky and Elaine, May, Dr. Kafka, and the men met in a room to discuss the next steps.

"Tom, have you downloaded anything else since we left?" asked Dr. Kafka.

"Nothing other than the goat Image I related earlier," answered Tom.

"Doc, is there something that might help stimulate his thought process?" asked Dr. Kafka.

"Nothing I can do here, but if we can find Tom's goat, that might stimulate another dump," replied the doctor.

"Maybe Dad needs to be talked to tonight," quipped Corky. "Maybe he's right," said Mary.

"Corky, would you and Elaine demonstrate to us old folks just what would be the best 'talking to' procedure we should use? But these beds are pretty well bolted to the floor, so you might not have the proper sound effects accompanying your talking-to demonstration."

"Mom," said both Elaine and Corky, "Please." "Well, I guess that unnatural shade of red in your face must need some medical aid," said Mary, with a twinkle in her eye.

"Doc, do you have anything to prescribe to help them?"

"From what I see, I would have to prescribe a course of treatment starting with a good night's bed rest and then review the results with a thorough physical exam in the morning."

At that point, nobody in the room could contain themselves any longer, and all burst into a round of laughter that resulted in the two of them turning a brighter shade of red.

"If these are the doctor's orders, then we shall have to follow them immediately," said Corky, grabbing Elaine's hand and leading her to their rooms.

Why me?

"You really are going to do a physical on them tomorrow, are you, Doc?" asked Tom, who was a bit slow on the uptake.

"Of course," said the Doc. "I should conduct it in front of their parents just to be sure it's thorough."

At that point, Tom's red face indicated he may need a physical. However, Mary stepped in and said, "If there is any physical therapy to be done, I will do it. Now, boys and girls, let's all get a good night's rest because the next time we go out, we probably will be roughing it. So, enjoy a good bed, hot food, and running hot water."

"At my expense," interjected Dr. Kafka. With that, they all said good night and left for their respective room, still chuckling.

The next morning, Elaine was up early for a run with a groggy Corky. She led them around the block, where they stopped at a small local coffee shop, trying to get a jump on waking up more before heading back for breakfast. The older woman behind the counter looked like she was about 100 years old, but had the smile of a 14-year-old that lit up the place every time she smiled, which was quite often.

"You are from out of town?" she asked as she poured a molasses-thick coffee into giant coffee mugs. "How'd you know," asked Elaine, not trusting Corky to say anything until he had his coffee, other than to mumble something incoherently.

"Your clothes and shoes are too new, and your accents are too refined. You are more like big city folks trying to blend in but don't know how."

"You got us," said Corky. "We're kinda on a honeymoon."

"Hornymoon," quipped Elaine, to which the woman replied, "In my day, we called it spooning and went camping because motels were too expensive."

"Well, we were trying to camp and some friends told us a great place to camp was by something called Goat Rock, but we couldn't find it on any map. Have you heard about it?"

"Sure have. In my younger days, we used to camp there. In those days, it was called Devil's Rock because the goat was a symbol for the devil. But the Chamber of Commerce changed it to Goat Rock so as not to scare off the tourist campers. Nowadays, much of the face of the mesa has fallen off so it no longer looks like anything, although there were some legends about mysterious lights at night. The Army sent out a detachment to investigate. They didn't find anything after several months of traipsing around up there. The Army had the parks department close down the area because several of their soldiers got hurt from the falling rocks. You want some more coffee to go with your pastry?"

"I'll have some more of both," said Corky, apparently finally rejoining the living from his earlier zombie state.

"I'll just have more coffee," said Elaine.

"How do you make it so strong?"

"That's the Moab special because during winter the city often gets cut off, so we make do until the roads clear. You don't throw out the coffee. You just add more grounds, and eventually the coffee improves to just the right thickness. We do have to occasionally throw out the grounds, but saving the coffee and adding a little water and more grounds will keep it at Moab consistency. Also, you don't necessarily have to clean your pot often, which helps to add to the taste," said the woman, showing a glass coffee pot that looked like it'd been painted black.

"For most tourists, we just give them regular coffee. But you two look like you needed the extra kick, so you got a cup of Moab."

"You are certainly right," said Elaine, who was starting to feel like she could run up Mount Everest.

"Is there still camping by Goat Rock? We would like to tell our friends that we did camp there for real."

"Sure," said the woman, "but I have to warn you it's dry camping. The only water is at the parking lot, which is the trailhead, so take several days' worth of water with you."

"So noted," said Corky. "Now, how do we get there?"

Later in the meeting room, while recounting their adventure in the coffee shop and sharing a gallon of Moab coffee with the others, Corky said, "The old woman said take Mill Creek Road off the 191 to Powerhouse Road. Follow it to the parking lot, which is also the trailhead. There is a side road over a narrow bridge over a dry creek, which is sometimes prone to flash flooding. Follow that dirt road for about five or 10 miles, then look up with your Imagination to your left, and you can see a wall that looks like some part of a goat's head. That's Goat Mountain. The best place to camp used to be about another two or three miles further on, but you'll know when you get there. Be careful not to camp under any overhanging rocks, but have fun." She also said that maybe we would see some of those mysterious lights she claimed that they used to see a long time ago.

After listening to their story, Dr. Kafka said, "That's interesting because I checked with the DOD, and they have no record of any military resources being deployed there other than the National Guard on a two-week summer training deployment near there."

"Satellite imaging doesn't show much but a lot of rocks, but there are some things that look like faint footpaths crisscrossing the area, which probably means we will spend a lot of time breaking in our new boots," said Elaine, looking up from her computer.

"Tom, have you dumped any new data yet?" asked Dr. Kafka.

"Maybe when we are in the area, but I can't count on it," confessed Tom.

"Well, it sounds like we will be camping for as long as a week, so we need our chefs to stock up appropriately. Corky, you and Bill find containers that will hold at least 7 gallons of water per person, so take the truck."

"Will do," said Bill, finally glad to have something to do. "Let's try to get things done by tonight so we can leave tomorrow morning before it starts to heat up. Before you go, here's a list of additional stuff we will need since we will be camping for a week," said Mary, calling on her scouting experience to fill in the gaps in their camping supplies and equipment.

After an exhaustive shopping trip, the team met back in Dr. Kafka's suite.

"Thank God for Army/Navy surplus stores," said Corky.

"We were able to find all the stuff for extended camping, including three large ice chests."

"We can fill them all," said Mary.

"I didn't know that Elaine was such a power shopper. We filled three grocery baskets in just under an hour. But the last items were harder to find in what is basically a dry county," said Mary, looking at Dr. K.

"We solved the water problem by finding 55-gallon drums with faucets that we will fill tomorrow just before we go out," said Bill.

"The same place where we got the water drums, we also found a long garden hose, so we won't have to ask to use the motel's equipment," said Bill.

"We can start filling the ice boxes tonight from the motel's ice machines and top off tomorrow, plus we can buy ice where we gas up," said Mary.

"Okay, Gang," said Dr. Kafka.

"We know where we are heading and what the schedules are. Let's plan on leaving by 0630 hours after breakfast across the street. We each will take a different route to Powerhouse Road and meet at the trailhead parking lot by 1100 hrs. Any questions? If not, let's get a good night's rest and that means everybody," said Dr. Kafka, looking pointedly at Bill, who groaned something about needing something to help him sleep.

Chapter 32

The next morning, Bill and Corky filled the water containers while Mary and May added ice to the ice chests. They covered their gear in the back of the truck with the tarp that Corky and Bill got at the surplus store. When each group finished their assigned tasks, they went across the street, had their last civilized breakfast, checked out, and left.

On the way out of town, each team topped off their gas tanks and filled several 5-gallon gas cans for each vehicle, just in case. Mary got two extra 25-pound bags of ice for the ice chests along with some "critical chocolate snacks." The trip to the trailhead took about two hours for each team to get there. Once all vehicles were there, they then put all vehicles into four-wheel drive and headed in the direction the old woman gave them.

Chapter 33

Mohammed met the pilot at the Moab airport the next morning. The leader reviewed the search area covered and established a level of confidence in their search procedure.

When asked if he had any additional info that might have helped narrow down the search, the leader replied that "our brothers across the way have been strangely quiet, so we are on our own until further notice."

He neglected to say that the site that received the information had been destroyed along with several "brothers" by drone hellfire missiles early yesterday. The surviving technical staff was trying to salvage what remained. But it would be three or four days before any assessment could be made and a new site established. His orders were to proceed to follow the Americans and acquire what they found.

The leader helped the pilot and his two observers to develop a grid search pattern with Moab at the center. The pilot took off around 1100 hrs. to search the Southwest quadrant, refueled, and had a light snack provided by the ever-present vending machines in the pilot's lounge, where the man and the woman were astounded by the variety of foodstuffs available. The search of the southeast quadrant was a bust. It consisted mostly of rock with no real discernible trails big enough for vehicles. The team returned to the base, refueled, and searched the northeast quadrant, and finally the northwest quadrant. If they found nothing the next day, they were to follow the same procedure using Salt Lake City as the center of their search pattern.

The pilot's two observers were much more rested after a good night's sleep and plenty of American food and coffee at a place called Starbucks. The takeoff was normal into a beautifully clear sky. For lunch, they returned to base to refuel and have a snack, where the woman remarked, "We've been in this country only four days," she said. "No wonder the Americans are so spoiled. They don't have to work for their food. They can just get it out of the machine."

To keep out of an argument, the pilot agreed with them, omitting the fact that one had to earn the money to put into the machines. After eating, they took off and returned to the southwest quadrant. Around 1500 hrs., their search pattern began at the farthest southern line of the grid. Again, the same scenery of rocks and sand. Around 1545 hrs., they reached the area of a trailhead. From there, they followed various faint dirt roads until the woman spotted what looked like a dust storm or dust devil on the horizon.

As they flew over, they spotted three cars and a truck driving north on a dirt road that appeared to be more dirt than road. The pilot called the leader on his cell phone and reported the position and direction of the convoy. He reported that the area was mostly rocks and looked very dry. He would return to base, backtracking, trying to find how to get to that road before they had to land at twilight.

That evening, the terrorists met in a room where everybody was staying for a planning session. It was decided that the group would need four SUVs with four-wheel drive, water, and foodstuffs. The leader next had to get funds added to his credit cards in order to acquire the needed equipment and supplies. Once that was done and verified, it was well into the next morning. Several groups were tasked with getting supplies and water for the 13 members of the group. The leader was able to rent four SUVs with four-wheel drive at a local car rental agency.

The leader figured it would take about 2 to 3 days to discover what the Americans were doing or had found. He then dispatched the pilot and his observers to shadow the American convoy. Finally, the group was able to leave and head for the trailhead. There, they were able, thanks to the pilot, to find the side road the Americans took. They followed the tracks left by the Americans for about 10 miles, then the tracks disappeared. The leader called the pilot for directions.

The pilot replied, "I've lost them, but that is the only road I can see, so I will keep following it."

The leader decided to stop for the night and ordered the group to camp. Because of poor planning, the men and women had to eat cold food and sleep on the ground with minimal protection from the cold in the blankets they stole from the motel. The next morning, they got on the road again with the pilot acting as eyes in the sky but still not finding anything.

Chapter 34

Once on the dirt road, or path as Bill described it, the team made good progress for the first 20 miles. Then they discovered what four-wheeling really means, driving across rock and riverbeds that were undermined with gopher burros that threatened to bog down even a four-wheel vehicle. The second time everybody almost got stuck, Dr. Kafka had Bill drive 100 yards ahead of the rest of them to make sure that it was passable for the convoy.

Bill said "Why me? Isn't there someone else you are willing to sacrifice?"

"No," said Dr. Kafka. "You have the most driving experience and if something happened to you, we would only be out a driver."

The hurt look that Bill gave Dr. Kafka was probably the finest acting anyone in the group had seen in quite some time.

"If I'm leading and concentrating on driving, I'll need another pair of eyes," he said, looking at May.

"Okay, I'll volunteer," said May.

"If for no other reason than to stop the whining and get this show on the road."

Bill tried to hide the smile on his face by suddenly developing a coughing fit.

"Water," he gasped.

"You'll get it after you get back in the car," said May.

Bill hopped quickly into the car knowing his five minutes of fame were over and it was time to get to work. About two hours later May radioed back that they had found a good spot for camping under some riverbed trees.

Several of the veterans on the team suggested that they pull well under the trees and add some camouflage to the cars to break up their outlines. They then took some branches, walked back about half a mile, and wiped out their tracks with those branches. Dr. Kafka said, "No tents and no campfires. Keep cooking to the minimum, and as much as it will pain me, we sleep on the ground." This last statement elicited a groan from Bill, who is very much a city boy, and camping ranks in his mind next to castor oil. Food was prepared, a guard schedule was set, and everybody turned in for the night.

Why me?

The next morning, as they were breaking camp, May heard a small plane approaching. "Let's stay undercover until he passes," said Dr. Kafka.

As the small plane flew over, Corky said, "I've seen that plane before. I think it might be connected with the trouble we've been having, but I'm not sure, and I don't have any way of checking."

"Well, I've been meaning to tell you all this; we have overwatch," said Dr. Kafka.

"Does that mean what I think it means?" said May.

"Yes," said Elaine.

"We have a satellite watching us. And how do we access it?" "What satellite?" said Dr. Kafka.

"But if there was one, you might try this frequency," he said, handing Elaine a small slip of paper. She then whipped out her computer and started trying to access a satellite.

"Elaine," said Dr. Kafka, "we only have about 20-minute viewing time every six hours, so take advantage of it while you can."

"Will do," replied Elaine.

"While on the subject of observation, did anybody get the tail number of that plane so I can call it in, just in case?" asked Dr. Kafka.

Corky did get the tail number and when Dr. Kafka called it in, he then announced that the plane was still sitting on the ground at Miami International.

"There must be some mistake," said May.

"Can you verify?" Dr. Kafka made another call, and 10 minutes later, he said the ground control and the tower at Miami airport had eyes on the plane sitting on the tarmac on the general aviation side of the airport.

"That must be how they have been able to keep track of us," said Tom.

"Well, let's get moving while I'll make another phone call," said Dr. Kafka.

Bill and May left first, then the rest of the team followed.

Chapter 35

The rest of the day was uneventful but was filled with some of the most wild and beautiful landscapes most of the team had ever seen. Even Bill remarked to May as they bounced along a particularly rocky portion of the trail.

"This is spectacular scenery. Are you saying you're starting to like the outdoors?" asked May.

"No, it's all just sand and rocks, but it's arranged artistically," was the reply by about 1600 hrs.

Mary looked very intently at the face of a wall of rock and excitedly called for a halt. I think we found it.

"Doesn't that look like some horns on the part of an animal," May said after carefully studying the mesa with a powerful set of binoculars.

Dr. Kafka said, "I think you are right. Let's find a place to camp and look around."

They ended up having to disperse vehicles over a relatively large area and cover them with the camouflage netting that Corky found at the Army/Navy surplus store. Some of the rock shapes looked like their tents, so hiding the tents was easy. The cooking area was a little harder, so the cooks used the tailgate of the truck and raised the camouflage netting higher over that area, which helped to further disguise the profile of the truck.

Once camp was set up, dinner was cooked. Even Dr. Kafka seemed to enjoy his steak, fried potatoes, and corn Niblett's, along with a glass of red wine. Dessert consisted of a tin of pralines and milk or water. After the meal, cleanup was done under Tom's supervision, who made sure everything was spotless, and all graywater was disposed of in a manner that would not attract any local vermin. Dr. Kafka then called the group together to plan the next day's activities and let everybody know that the mysterious plane would not be bothering them. He gave no further details. Elaine was able to access the satellite again but detected nothing on this pass. The group turned in at dark with Mary checking on Tom to see if anything new had decoded in his head. "Nothing yet," said Tom. The camp quieted down with two guards on watch from concealed locations throughout the night.

The next morning, after a scrumptious breakfast of pancakes, eggs, bacon, and coffee, Dr. Kafka divided the group into teams of three, with team one guarding the camp.

Why me?

Bill, May, and the Dr. on one team. Corky, Martha, and Mary made another. Dr. Kafka, Tom, and Andy make the third team, with the extra security people forming the fourth group. The teams would report back to camp in four hours to eat, rest, and relieve the team guarding the camp.

Chapter 36

The next morning, the pilot found fire trucks by the burned-out hulk of his plane.

"What happened?" he asked.

"As near as we can tell, some terrorists tossed a Molotov cocktail at this plane while it was being fueled. Luckily, the driver managed to put the fire out at the fuel truck, but we couldn't save the plane," said the fire captain.

When the pilot contacted the leader about the destruction of his plane, the leader asked, "How soon can you get another plane?"

"I can get a rental but if they check my credentials, I would be reported and probably arrested."

"Is there another way you can obtain one instead of renting?" replied the leader. (Translated, can you steal one?)

"Acquiring a plane isn't like acquiring a car," replied the pilot.

"Airports are closely monitored now due to drug dealers stealing planes to ferry drugs, so it is much more difficult to even get on an airfield," said the pilot.

"We need you in the air for the next two days," said the leader.

"I don't care how you do it; just get in the air."

"Okay, will try," said the pilot well aware of the leaders' lack of knowledge about the technical side of aviation. Maybe, just maybe, he could find a local looking to pick up some extra money by renting out his plane to get some "aerial photos" of possible routes to be built through the pilot. After he hung up and disposed of the phone, he started scanning the for-sale ads in the general aviation pilots' lounge.

Chapter 37

After the leader hung up, he called the group together. "Brothers, we are near the infidels we seek. I can feel that we must be cautious that they do not detect us. So, one car will travel ahead of the rest of us. We will follow very slowly to keep the dust down that would give us away. When you find them, just keep going until you're out of sight. Then, wait until we give the signal to attack. This way we can attack from two sides and gain whatever they have found. Our pilot lost his plane, so we are without air cover until he can find another. But with Allah's blessing, we will succeed." A man and woman were selected and left in the first car. They would appear to be less threatening to anyone they came across by pretending to be scouting for campgrounds. After 15 minutes, the rest followed behind them.

That morning, Dr. K divided the area into search grids. The teams then left to search their assigned areas, leaving Elaine back at camp with Dr. Kafka and Tom to coordinate the search teams and for Elaine to check the satellite coverage when available. Tom began to wander around the immediate area to see if he could get a data dump. Around

1000 hrs., when Elaine checked the satellite, she said, "Oh, oh. This looks suspicious..."

"What do you mean?" said Dr. Kafka.

"There are three cars about 20 miles away, but one looks like it left the group and is headed this way. The other two cars are still parked, damn! Just lost SAT coverage, so I will have to wait for the next pass."

"What do you think?" asked Dr. Kafka.

"Should we call the teams back?"

"No, not all of them. I would call team 4 back to have some extra manpower to station up in those rocks just in case," said Elaine. Since several of those guys on that team are Afghan vets, they know how to best disperse themselves." When team four returned to the base, Elaine briefed them that a group of unknowns was headed this way. Dr. Kafka then called the other teams and advised them to keep their heads down until we have more info as to the unknowns and their intentions, but we have to assume that they are hostile.

When Team 4 returned, they immediately removed heavier firepower from the truck and proceeded to conceal themselves in various rocks above the camp. About 45 minutes later, the lookout reported seeing a single car driving very slowly out on the road. Dr. Kafka, Mary, and Tom seated themselves at a table so that when the car finally reached the camp, they would appear to be just having a cup of coffee. As the car reached the camp, it stopped, and the man asked how far up the road was another camping area.

"The road goes for another 15 or more miles, but there is a very nice camping area about 20 miles up ahead by the river."

"Thanks," said the man as he got in the car with the woman and slowly headed up the road.

"What do you think," asked Dr. K when the car was finally out of sight.

"That woman looks so nervous. I thought she was going to ask to use our latrine," said Mary.

"I agree, and did you notice how the man's eyes constantly were looking around our camp? I think we need to call in our other teams, just in case," said Dr. Kafka. "Will do," said Elaine.

The car with the couple drove for 2 miles until they were out of sight, then stopped and reported to the leader what they had seen. They then waited for further directions.

Why me?

After the leader hung up, he called the group together. "Brothers, when our pilot, with Allah's guidance, finds the infidels, we will follow and capture what they find. But we must wait until they find something."

"How do you know where to look?" asked one of the group leaders.

"Feelings are good, but facts are better."

The leader looked at the man, thinking about when to eliminate him since I can't have my authority questioned, he thought. But he said, "Our brothers at home decoded a longitude address, and that line passes very close to Moab, where we will position our group to await further information."

"Thank you," said the man, not knowing he would not see the next sunrise. The leader then turned to the group and said, "Pack up and let's get to Moab."

He then left to settle their bill with the motel. The trip to Moab was uneventful, but several of the men remarked that the desert reminded them of their homes in Afghanistan. "Don't worry," said the leader.

"We will be home soon...one way or another," he thought.

In Moab, they found a cheap motel near several fast-food places. To the peasants in the group, they were living like sultans with endless eating options, sleeping in rooms with clean sheets and soft beds and an endless supply of, praise Allah, ice and air conditioning. The next morning, the leader gave each person $10 American to go get breakfast at one of the fast-food places. The new men's and women's English wasn't very good, so they were assigned to a person who did speak and read English.

At the fast-food places, each group took a very long time to order as they had to have the menus explained to them. They found out that the hamburger wasn't made with swine but a cow. However, many of the breakfast offerings of egg McMuffins or sausage in each biscuit were made with pork, which they avoided due to religious beliefs. The group thought the food was good, but the coffee was very weak compared to what they were used to drinking back home.

After breakfast they waited in their rooms until summoned by the leader. When the leader had eaten, he made a call that was routed through a dummy number in the U.S. to an international number, which was then routed to his contact back home. He learned they had been unable to make much further progress on the data he sent them. His contact also warned him not to contact him anymore. He would be contacted when and if they had anything of importance to report. After the leader hung up and destroyed his phone, he had another chore to do. He summoned the man who spoke up last night to drive him to "check out the area." They first drove up into the mountains surrounding the town, where the leader had the man stop the car on a high bluff overlooking Moab. He had the man get the binoculars from the car and then used them to look around for a minute. He then gave the man the binoculars and pointed to an area west of the airport. "Tell me what you see," he said.

When the man looked, the leader said, "You're looking in the wrong area. Look there," he said, stepping behind the man and placing his hands on both sides of the man's head.

The man, sensing something, started to put the binoculars down and turn to the leader. But it was too late as the leader pushed the man over the edge of the cliff. The man tossed the binoculars up, trying to regain his balance. He almost succeeded, but gravity won, and the man went over the edge to his death, falling into a small ravine 500 feet below. The leader caught the binoculars by their strap before they fell over the edge. He then cautiously checked over the side but couldn't see the man's body.

"With any luck, it would be days before anyone finds him," thought the leader.

Then, taking one last look around, he got into the car and drove back to town. When Mohammed got back, the man's team leader asked where was the man he saw the leader leave with?

The leader replied, "He's on a special assignment and will join us later."

The man's team leader, a woman, had been in the organization for several years and had learned that very few people return from the leader's "special assignments." But she thought that to herself. Mohammed went to his room, called the front desk, and explained what he was looking for. About an hour later, a youngish woman in her late 20s knocked on the door. Inside, she was "interrogated" for the next several hours. When She left later, she was holding a washcloth to a split lip and a roll of bills clutched in her other hand.

Later that day, Mohammed received a phone call and then called the group leaders together. "Brothers, have your men rest and be ready to leave any time in the morning as soon as our pilot spots the bastard infidels. Since we will probably be going into the surrounding terrain, pick up some water and enough food for a couple of days. Get a few blankets or sleeping bags in case we get to sleep under the heavens. Be sure to have your men check their guns and sharpen their knives for use later. Now go, and may Allah guide your way."

As the three remaining leaders got up to leave, one stopped to ask, "Will more brothers be here to replace our fallen?"

"No," said the leader.

"Allah has helped us weed out the lesser warriors, so now we have the chosen ones to complete our mission."

Outside, one of the team leaders turned to the other two and said, "You've seen these dogs fight. I would prefer to have more men, but we won't, so I will personally check each person's weapon and review tactics. Plus, tomorrow, I will have them carry all the ammunition they can carry."

"Agreed," said the other two team leaders.

The next morning, the leader checked that everyone had eaten a substantial breakfast, gassed up the cars, and packed them to be ready to leave on a moment's notice.

The person the pilot called said he would rent his Cessna 182 out for $200 an hour and, assuming the check ride was good; the pilot would have to refill the tanks and pay for any oil needed. Of course, any damage would be extra. The pilot showed his fake credentials, took the check ride, and signed a document saying the plane was in good shape and the rate was $200 an hour. The pilot topped off the tanks, ran the checklist, and took off. His observer crew had left to replace some of the missing fighters lost in previous contacts with the Americans. A side benefit of not having the extra weight of the two observers was that he burned less fuel and could stay airborne longer. Since he had already searched both sides of Road 119, he expanded the grid another 20 miles. After searching the west side of 119 for a distance of 50 miles from Moab, he landed and refueled. After a light lunch from one of the machines in the general aviation lounge at the Moab airport, he began searching the east side of 119. About an hour into his search, he spotted a group of two cars and one truck just leaving a parking lot and heading off on a dirt road to the northeast. He flew on ahead of the caravan for about 10 miles and didn't see any turnoffs, so he assumed they would have to keep on that path for a while. He phoned this information to the terrorist leader, who got his group moving to the parking lot the pilot had located. They followed the designated road for the next two hours until it was getting dark. Knowing how fast the darkness falls in the mountainous areas, the leader had them pull off the road and set up camp for the night. The next morning, the pilot took off and flew over the terrorist camp, then followed the road ahead of them. He spotted the Americans about 25 miles ahead of his people. He phoned the information to the leader. After the leader hung up, he made another call and then called the group together.

"Brothers, we are near the infidels we seek. I can feel it, so we must be cautious that they do not detect us."

Chapter 38

The leader divided his remaining group. One unit would attack from the front and distract the infidels, while the second group would attack from the west side. The third group, consisting of the man and woman who were waiting, would attack from behind. He ordered all groups to take four hours to rest, hydrate, and eat some food. All weapons needed to be checked and ammunition distributed. It was decided that one car would travel ahead out of sight of the rest of everyone else.

The man and woman who were selected left in the first car. They would appear to be less threatening to anyone they came across. Their cover was to be a couple scouting for a campground. After about 15 minutes, the rest will follow behind them. The appointed couple got into their car and left.

"Looks like they're getting ready to do something," said Elaine, looking up from her computer screen. "When will the satellite be in range next?" asked Dr. Kafka. "About five hours," said Elaine. "Not good," said Dr. Kafka. "We need more intel. Let's see if we still have any friends in high places," he said, picking up his SAT phone. A few minutes later, Dr. Kafka recalled everybody to camp. As they sat around eating lunch, Dr. Kafka explained the situation to them.

"We have hostiles on the road in front and in back. Our next satellite pass will be in 4 ½ hours, but it looks like something will happen before we will have eyes in the sky. We need to monitor in real-time at least the groups in front of us and behind us. Any suggestions?"

One of the veterans raised his hand and asked, "Why not just send out some scouts to keep an eye on them?"

"That's a great idea," said Dr. Kafka, "But they are 15 miles away over open ground. Also, we don't know what happened to the couple supposedly looking for a campground. So, the possibility exists that we have bad guys and gals in front of and behind us. Sending out observers would reduce our firepower significantly, and since our phones don't work, we have only our radios and those will not carry very far reliably. Any other ideas?"

They discussed several ideas and finally decided to post two snipers as high as they could get above the camp. The rest of the group will take various concealed positions surrounding the camp with a fallback, last-stand position that would allow them to defend long enough to discourage a prolonged attack. Each team member then supplied his or her position with extra water and ammo.

Dr. Kafka developed a rotating schedule, allowing one-third of the group to get food and rest at a time. The snipers would be supplied with MREs, so they wouldn't have to spend time and effort climbing up and down from their positions.

As each person went to his or her assigned position, Tom said to Dr. Kafka, "You haven't assigned me. Where do you want me to go?"

Dr. Kafka replied, "You'll be with me in the fallback position. Our job will be to ensure the others have a clear path to retreat through if necessary. Hopefully you might get a brain dump that will be useful to our situation. Now, let's take extra first-aid kits and ammo up to the stronghold just in case they are needed."

Just then, Dr. Kafka's SAT phone buzzed. Dr. Kafka looked at the caller's ID and then said, "I hope you have some good news." As he was listening, Tom began loading up backpacks with the needed supplies. When he was finished with the call, Dr. Kafka put down the phone. "Anything?"

Why me?

"Good news and bad news. The Utah National Guard will be sending some help. The bad news is that it will be at least three or more hours before they get here."

Tom said, "I hope we have that much time."

"So do I," said Dr. K.

Chapter 39

"Let's review the plan one last time," said Mohammed.

"Group 2 will take an assault position over towards those rocks on the west. You will wait and attack from the road. After group 2 attacks, group 3 will then attack from behind. Any questions? None good. Notify group 3 to get into attack position and wait on my command. Now move to your positions, and may our Lord be with you."

The pilot topped off his tanks and took off, headed toward the battle. He informed the leader of his ETA, and the leader updated him on the attack plan. He was to overfly the infidels' position and relay information about their locations. Mohammed then called the information to the attack groups so they could better plan their attack approach. On the overflight, the pilot could barely make out the concealed Americans. He informed the leader, neglecting to mention the two snipers. The pilot then made a phone call using an SAT phone he had just for this purpose.

Chapter 40

Dr. Kafka and Tom were scanning their surroundings while hiding from the small plane circling above. Suddenly, Dr. Kafka's SAT phone buzzed. Dr. Kafka looked at the caller ID with a puzzled look on his face.

"What's that?" said Tom.

"Not sure," said Dr. Kafka.

"It says to call this number but doesn't say who it is."

"Are you going to call it?" said Tom.

"Might as well," said Dr. Kafka, dialing the number.

When the line was answered, the person who answered said, "Are you the Americans in the rocks?"

"Who are you, and what is that noise," said Dr. Kafka.

"Are you in a boat somewhere?"

"Kind of," said the voice.

"I'm in a motorboat of the sky. I'm in the plane above you. I thought you would like to know that there are three groups getting ready to attack your positions. They know your positions but do not know about the two people high above you."

"Who are you?" asked Dr. Kafka, "and how did you get this number?"

"Let's just say it's nice to repay you a little bit for all the support you have given us since 1948. But enough talking. I need to take this plane out of the picture. I will buzz you, then have the engine trouble."

"Wait," said Dr. Kafka.

"Where are these groups?"

"One on the road in front of you, one on the road in back of you, and one to the west of you. Good luck."

At that point, the small plane stopped circling and drove down toward their positions. As it passed over their heads, they heard the sounds of gunfire then the engine started smoking.

The pilot put his 9 mm Glock on the seat beside him and radioed the leader, "I'm hit and going down."

"May Allah be with you," said the leader.

"And God be with me," thought the Mossad agent as he banked hard, hoping to reach the campground by the river behind the Americans' position.

Suddenly, the engine burst into flames, forcing the pilot to set the plane down sooner than planned. As he touched down, rocks tore at the undercarriage, immediately causing the plane to nose over. The front of the plane burst into flame. The pilot struggled to free himself before the flames reached him. As the soles of his shoes started melting, he managed to get the door open and started crawling away when the plane exploded with a whoosh, sending flames and burning gas into the air.

He almost reached safety when a shower of burning gas fell across his legs. He struggled to crawl those last few feet in agony with fire on the backs of his legs. He finally was able to weakly turn over and put out the flames. He thought just before he passed out, "There goes my running game."

After the cryptic phone call, Dr. Kafka radioed the teams to find different locations but to stay low. Snipers stay put.

"What was that all about?" asked Tom.

"It seems like we had an angel looking over us. He told me that there was a third group off to the west. Unfortunately, that means that I don't have anybody left to cover it. Guess what?"

"You mean?" said Tom, "Yep," said Dr. Kafka, picking up some extra water.

"With the plane gone, you and I can sneak over there and set up on those rocks."

The boss got on the radio and informed the teams that they were moving to cover the group coming from the West, and as they were moving, the first shots from the road started hitting the rocks where team members had been. But thanks to the pilot, they had moved.

Chapter 41

Because of poor training, several in the terrorist group believed that just hosing the area with automatic fire killed the enemy, and since there was no return fire, they began to advance carelessly. When the agents finally returned fire, one terrorist was killed outright, and three were seriously wounded, leaving two of the more experienced fighters and the leader still able to return effective fire. Unfortunately, one American was severely wounded and would die within the hour. The west group began attacking, thinking their approach was not covered, counting on their surprise attack to wipe out most of the Americans. Unfortunately, three terrorists were killed before they realized that this side was protected. The only casualty from the American side was Tom, who was bleeding from being hit with a few rock fragments chipped by glancing bullets.

The leader then called the rear group to attack. Both were wiped out by a sniper before the rear defensive group could fire. Then, the battle settled into a kind of stalemate, with both sides down to about the same number of people still capable of fighting. One more American was killed along with the sniper who took out the attacking couple in the rear. To break the current stalemate, Dr. Kafka had the rear group join Tom and him to take out the remaining terrorists in the west. As soon as Tom and Dr. Kafka were reinforced with the rear group, they started moving toward the retreating terrorists. Suddenly, a grenade appeared, almost floating in the sky.

"Grenade!" yelled one of the agents.

Everybody immediately dived behind whatever cover they could find. Tom ducked behind a large boulder only to fall through.

"What the hell," exclaimed Tom just as the grenade went off with a loud bang. His last thought before passing out from a terrific bump on the head from a piece of shrapnel was, "Why me?"

Chapter 42

"Tom, where are you?" called Mary.

"It is so quiet," thought Tom.

"I must be deaf from the blast, yet why can I hear Mary?"

As he tried to respond, he realized he was face down on the ground with a terrific headache. As he tried to turn over, he let out a loud groan.

"I hear you," said Mary, "but where are you?"

"Here," moaned Tom. He finally managed to turn over and opened his eyes. When he tried to look around, he noticed everything appeared hazy.

"Must have affected my eyes," he thought. He tried calling out, "I'm here." He thought he could see Mary and Corky.

"Where are you?" said Corky.

"Over here to your left. Are you blind?" They both turned toward the sound of Tom's voice.

"Where?" said Corky. Finally, Tom managed to sit up and look around more fully.

He seemed to be sitting on a stair that led up to the wall of the mountain. He turned and looked at Mary and Corky. They were looking right at him.

"Tom, we can hear you. Where are you, Honey?" said Mary. He finally realized that he was somehow hidden in plain sight. He tried to stand, accompanied by many groans. He finally started stumbling toward them.

Corky and Mary were looking for the sounds of groaning when suddenly a macabre apparition appeared, covered in blood, stumbling toward them. As Mary rushed toward him, she caught him just as he started to collapse and eased him onto the ground. As Corky rushed up, he took one look and called for a medic.

Chapter 43

Tom came to and immediately noted two things. First, he had the mother of headaches, worse than he could remember from his college days. Second, the noise level surrounding him was unreal. The noise included cars, trucks, something sounding like a helicopter, and shouting in multiple voices, all of which were so loud that he started groaning in pain.

As he tried to open his eyes, a familiar voice said, "You're alive." As his eyes adjusted to the light, he noticed his head resting on a soft, warm pillow. As he began to focus more on the surroundings, he looked up and saw a welcome sight. As Mary's face came into focus, she was looking down at him with a big smile. The soft pillow was on her lap. His eyes moved around, and he saw May sitting beside him, her arm in a sling. As he became more awake, the noise level went down to a more tolerable level.

Tom looked up at Mary and said, "What happened? The last thing I remember is diving into a rock. But that's impossible. What did happen? And what's going on? Who or what is making all that noise?"

May interjected, "Is he going to be okay? He looks awful."

"He's waking up and is coming back to us," said Mary, also thinking she needs to work with May's bedside manner.

As Tom struggled to sit up with Mary and May's help, Mary updated him with, "Yes, you did dive into a rock to avoid a grenade a bad person threw at us. It looks like you got hit by a piece of rock on the side of your head. As you know, any cut to the head area bleeds like crazy. Remember when Corky cut his head on something while snooping around in the garage when he was young? You were teaching at the time, so I had to take him to the ER. He got four stitches and was so proud of them and couldn't wait until you got home to show you."

"Yeah... Kind of," mumbled Tom, slowly gaining more functioning.

"Well, dear, you can brag that you beat him with five stitches. The noise is the National Guard who arrived in three helicopters. Dr. Kafka didn't tell them exactly what was needed, so they brought everything, including several medics, one who sewed you up. When they arrived, they caught the rest of the terrorists and are interrogating them as politely as the Army knows how."

Her statement was punctuated by a scream that seemed out of place amid the rest of the noise surrounding them. As Tom was absorbing all this, he looked at May.

"Are you okay?"

"It seems I need to pick better places to dive when someone throws a grenade at me. I hit my shoulder on a rock, but Doc says nothing broken, just bruised."

"What about the rest of us?" asked Tom.

"Is he awake asked a gruff voice?"

"Yes," said May.

"Is he okay?" asked Dr. Kafka.

"I won't know until tonight," said Mary with that familiar twinkle in her eye.

"You know what I mean," said Dr. Kafka, trying to muffle a small laugh. Tom was always a little slow picking up on certain things but finally caught on and started to chuckle. And then was immediately hit with a piercing pain in his head and groaned out loud.

Mary said, "You have a concussion, Dear, and will probably have a headache for a while. The doc gave me these to give to you if you need them," she said, handing two white pills and a bottle of water, both of which Tom downed immediately.

While waiting for the medication to kick in, Tom asked Dr. Kafka, "What's our status?"

Dr. Kafka gave one of his very few smiles and said, "You found the entrance when you dived into that rock. The National Guard is mopping up and has set up a security ring around the area. We went up to the door in the face of the cliff, and that was as far as we got. We were waiting for you to finish your beauty sleep to see if you know how to get in, do you?"

"I have no idea," said Tom.

"I'm surrounded by beautiful women beckoning to my every whim. The medication is great, and I'm not getting shot at or bombed, so why would I want to change and go looking at the wall of a cliff?"

May smiled and said, "That's the first time anybody has called me beautiful that was not trying to get me into bed with them."

"Hush, child," said Mary.

"That's my job." Another round of chuckling finally did release a lot of tension for the group.

"If you all can stop sounding like Bill, can we focus on getting the door open, that is, if Tom is up to it?"

"I don't know, Dr. Kafka. I just am a little hazy."

At which point Mary interjected, "He needs to rest so he will get some rest, and then I might let you talk to him."

"You don't need to mother him," said Corky to the woman who was responsible for taking out two terrorists and who pulled a wounded agent to safety amid a hail of gunfire.

"I'm not being soft on him. He was wounded and needs to be in good shape for what I'm sure Dr. Kafka will be trying to put him through. As his official bodyguard charged with his Health & Safety, I agree with her," said May.

"Okay," said Dr. Kafka.

"We can start in the morning if that is okay with his bodyguards. The guard brought in some inflatable huts instead of tents so we could rest there for the evening. Mary, do you think you can whip up some grub for our team while I need to ask the guard for some of their rations?"

"Not a problem," said Mary, already planning a victory meal.

"Let me get with Elaine and see what we can do."

"Okay, we rest tonight and get started at first light."

"No," said Mary.

"We are retired so we can start after 8 a.m. and breakfast."

"Who's running this outfit?" said Dr. Kafka.

"Boss," interrupted Tom.

"Can I talk to you privately?" After everybody backed off, although Mary was still within visual range, Tom said to Dr. Kafka, "I gave into the alpha leader years ago, and my life became a whole lot nicer. I suggest you bend a little. Whatever is in there has been there for over 80 years that we know of. A few more hours should not make a difference."

"Okay," said Dr. Kafka.

"I have reporting to do, and someone will have to start spinning a story to account for what's going on."

With that Dr. Kafka walked away only to be intercepted by a guard captain. "Sir, the Colonel asked me to check to see if you knew anything about a plane crash about 15 miles out that way," he said, pointing toward the north.

"A Park Ranger found a burned-out plane and the pilot who was mumbling in some foreign language. His legs were badly burned, and our doctors don't know if they can save them."

"Son," said Dr. Kafka, "give that man everything he needs. If he can be transported to Walter Reed, arrange it. If not, tell me who are the top doctors in this country for treating his type of wounds and I'll have them here in 18 hours."

"Wow, who is he?" asked the captain.

"I don't know. But he probably saved our lives, so get on it and let me know what you need. The same goes for any of the wounded, including your people."

"Thank you, Sir," said the captain.

"We take care of our own. But I will relay your offer to the Colonel."

With that, he saluted, turned, and left. Dr. Kafka almost automatically returned his salute but figured the fact that he was a two-star general in the Air Force reserve didn't need to be broadcast.

That night, Mary, May, and Martha produced not a meal but a banquet. Mary talked to one of the helicopter pilots and arranged with them to bring certain supplies that she had Elaine had ordered through her computer that the guard had graciously tied into their network. With the help of some of the guard soldiers who just happened to be chefs in their day jobs, they produced prime rib roast, rack of lamb, and boiled shrimp. Garlic mashed potatoes, and local vegetables in a cream sauce rounded off the meal. The dessert turned out to be apple pie with ice cream. The guard provided ovens, and Mary learned that the Army had changed meal prep over the years.

With modern equipment, a very complete kitchen could be transported on a single pallet which these boys claimed needed to be tested periodically to make sure everything was in working condition, and this was a good opportunity to test it. Beverages for the civilians were provided by the Colonel, who happened to own a winery nearby. The guard soldiers had soda, coffee and somehow beer, even though they were on deployment. The wine was very good, and Dr. Kafka quietly ordered several cases to be shipped to his home.

While everyone was well-fed, Tom ate very little due to some remaining nausea from the concussion. Mary made sure he did eat some of everything to keep the doctor from the guard talking about putting Tom under observation under proper conditions in a proper hospital. Tom finally settled down to sleep that night after two more of those little pain pills. The doctor didn't tell Mary that those pills were restricted because they cost almost as much as his first car.

Chapter 44

The next morning a gourmet breakfast was prepared by the guard cooks that consisted of eggs Benedict, fresh fruit, hash browns, and hot coffee made with beans grown on a very small local farm. When Elaine tried to find out where to get more of those coffee beans because Corky thought it was the best coffee he had ever tasted, Elaine found out that locally, in Utah terms, meant within 100 miles. You also needed a referral and a big wallet to get even a small amount of the beans.

Fortunately, Dr. Kafka was able to alleviate her disappointment. Of course, they would have to name their firstborn after Dr. Kafka in exchange for the favor. After careful consideration for five seconds, Elaine agreed. That was how 2 pounds of the gourmet coffee beans appeared under the family Christmas tree with their names on it that Christmas.

After breakfast and with the doctor's reluctant approval, Tom was released from his bed to go to the wall. The guard had packed up everything, including the kitchen, which Mary watched with a great deal of regret but vowed to obtain her own for future family outings.

Why me?

The Colonel left a few guardsmen to ensure their privacy, but the rest of them packed up and left. During breakfast, Dr. Kafka asked Tom if he had had any more brain dumps, and Tom said, "no." So, Dr. Kafka let the topic rest. After the meal, Tom went to the rock. Corky demonstrated the unique properties of the holographic rock. Elaine said she wasn't sure if the U.S. had that kind of technology but would check when she had time. Secretly, Dr. Kafka had checked last night and the answer was that not any country could produce and power that type of hologram.

Once they were inside the rock, a stone path between the rocks led to the seemingly blank wall of the plateau.

"We tried to open it last night but couldn't even find a door," said Dr. Kafka.

"We hoped that we would have better luck during daylight but still can't see any way inside or even if there is an entrance. So spread out and look around. Corky and Elaine, you start at that end," said Dr. Kafka, pointing to the left.

"Bill you and May take that end. Tom and Mary check the pathway for something we have missed. Martha and I will scan the face here and see if we can find any sign of an opening."

After about 30 minutes and finding nothing, each group returned. As Tom was returning, he stumbled and was caught by Mary.

"What happened?" asked Mary, worried that Tom was having a relapse.

"I'm okay," said Tom.

"I just had a partial dump. Look for a small rock shaped like a pyramid," he said.

"It's over here," said Elaine.

"I almost picked it up for souvenir."

"Well, pick it up and put it in that small depression next to it."

"I don't see one," said Elaine.

"It's got to be there," said Tom.

"It may be covered over, but it's near that rock."

The rest of the group converged on the area and started gently brushing the surface dirt to expose the rock surface underneath.

"I think I've got something," said Martha.

She began carefully brushing dirt from a slight round depression.

"I don't think that's it," said Dr. Kafka.

"That's round and the rock is a triangular shape. You would expect them to match, wouldn't you?"

"Let me try," said Elaine, moving the rock to the depression.

"Well, it fits, but nothing is happening," was Dr. Kafka's observation.

"I don't know," said Corky, looking at the face of the mesa.

"If you look closely, you can see a small square outlined with white."

"The question is now, what do we do?" asked Mary.

"It should open," said Tom. Corky pressed all around it on the square and nothing happened.

May said, "There is a small, raised surface over here."

"Can you press it, or does it move in any way?" asked Dr. Kafka.

May pressed the protrusion, and the cover of the square popped up, revealing an old-fashioned alphanumeric pad with various symbols on it instead of numbers. As Corky started to touch it, Tom interjected, "I remember that there is a warning that there is a detection system built-in that cost the lives of several technicians trying to work out the combination."

Corky jumped back. The group studied the keypad, each of whom was hoping for some sort of inspiration when Bill asked, "Are any of the pads worn?"

"Why do you ask that," said May.

"Well, sometimes when I would visit my 'friends,' the doors would be closed. I was too embarrassed to call up to have them let me in, plus it would spoil the surprise of my being there. But if you look closely at the pads, the keys that were worn were the combination. And most places only used four numbers, no doubt to make it easy on the old folks to remember," he said, looking at Dr. Kafka, who snorted and said, "The same old folks who write your paycheck you mean?"

At which point Tom said, "Can we just focus for a minute?"

"Okay," said May, looking very closely at the keypad.

"The only one that might be worn is this one. What do you think, Bill," said May.

Bill squinted and said, "I think you're right; that's the only one that appears worn. It seems there should be others, but should I go ahead and press the worn one?" said Bill.

"Okay," said Dr. Kafka.

"Let's stand back. Is there a stick or rod we can use to press it?"

"I've got a knife," said May, producing a small stiletto.

"I would rather you use something nonmetallic, if possible," said Dr. Kafka.

"How about this," said Corky, producing a small piece of petrified limb.

"That'll do," said Dr. Kafka.

"Let's all stand back while Corky goes ahead."

Corky stepped off to one side of the pad and reached around to press the button with a stick. The result was almost anti-climactic. A hidden door quietly opened and glowed with a slightly orange tint illuminating a short passageway ending in another door.

"Corky, you opened it, you, you have the honor," said Dr. Kafka.

"Okay," said Corky, stepping into the passageway. He cautiously walked to the door at the end and said, "There is a kind of odd-shaped handle about the middle of the door. Shall I give it a try?"

"Go ahead," said Dr. Kafka, watching from the outside. Corky tugged and turned the handle. Nothing happened.

"It won't open," said Corky.

"Try pushing on it," said Mary.

"Okay," said Corky, pushing on the handle and almost falling on his face as the door quickly opened. Lights snapped on, illuminating a large room with several openings around the walls.

The center of the room held a desk-like piece of furniture with an odd-shaped chair. The room appeared to be some sort of a reception area. At that point, the rest of the team could no longer keep out. They all rushed in, crowding around Corky, who was studying a screen behind the desk.

Chapter 45

The screen had six groups of symbols, with each group written in a different color. May looked from the screen and then around the room. It appeared to be roughly triangular-shaped, with six exits, including the one they came through. Not all doorways were rectangular in shape, but were more triangular-shaped and appeared closed or blocked. The ceiling, she guessed, was about 20 or more feet above the floor. The walls in the room had light panels that glowed with a slightly orange tint, like in the entranceway. Corky looked around and asked the "duh" question. What is the power source? There are no obvious power lines anywhere in the area.

Mary chimed in, "This place is cleaner than any place I have ever been in, and the air smells fresh, kind of like on a mountain meadow."

Mary turned to Tom, "What is this place? Do you remember or know about it?"

"No," said Tom. "I got nothing, how about you?"

She then asked Dr. Kafka, who replied, "I had no inkling of what we're seeing. I expected to find a small research facility, probably in an abandoned mine. Does this look like an abandoned mineshaft?" he asked May.

"If this place had been built by the us, then somebody used technology not available to any of the projects I worked on. Take that screen over there. We didn't use that type of smart screen until the early 80s, which probably means the government had it 10 years earlier. But Tom was already out of the service by the late 70s. He probably was uploaded in the early to mid-60s, based on some of the dates on the paperwork generated during one of his dumps."

"Well, look at this keyboard," said Elaine, sitting down in the odd-shaped chair behind the desk.

"This is not a standard QWERTY keyboard. In fact, there are no letters or numbers on it," she said, pulling the keyboard out of its niche on the desk.

"What did you do?" said Corky.

"What do you mean?" said Elaine.

"Whatever you did just made this screen start to glow."

"I just moved the keyboard closer to better see the symbols," said Elaine, turning to look at the screen. As she turned back to the keyboard, she uttered a startled, "What!"

As the group turned towards her, they saw that a small holographic projection of the screen behind her had appeared over the keyboard.

"This is cool," she muttered, then turned to look at Dr. Kafka and said, "Can I have one of these, please?"

"Me, too," said Corky.

"Try hitting one of the symbols," said Corky.

"Wait a minute," said Dr. Kafka, "We don't know anything about the symbols or what they do. We need to get some linguists in here."

"Too late," said Elaine, hitting one key in the middle of the keyboard.

The same symbol appeared on both screens. "That's enough," said Dr. Kafka. "Let's spread out and search the place. Also, check to see if any of those doors open. Okay, now get moving."

The group began to check out the room more systematically, with each team checking a different door and trying to open the doors without any luck. The doors had no handles and fitted so well into their frames that Bill could not fit his pocketknife blade between the frame and the doors. After 15 minutes, they were grouped around the desk.

"No luck," said each team.

"The only door that would open is the one we came in, and it has a handle on it, not like these other doors that have no handles," said Martha.

"Well, there's got to be a way in. We're just missing something. All doors must have a way to open them," said Bill.

"What if they are not doors but something else? What if these entrances were sealed for a reason? Maybe there was some biological or deadly radiation behind them. We don't have enough information," Bill said.

"We need to do a better job and need to rest. Let's have the guards set up a perimeter, get some food, and rest. Then bring in the equipment to explore this room and its secrets right and proper," said Dr. Kafka.

Why me?

Reluctantly, they all adjourned. Mary and Elaine got with Martha to prepare some food. Nobody claimed to be hungry. Yet when the seafood gumbo began cooking, everybody, including the few guardsmen, began to hover around the kitchen.

When the food was ready, the doctor, who was both a medical and security backup, proclaimed he had to pass judgment on the food, medically, of course. And because he was from Louisiana, he would make sure the cooks weren't trying to poison anybody with inferior southern food. He cautiously dipped his spoon into his bowl, sniffed the spoonful professionally, and then cautiously sampled the spoonful of deliciously looking stew. He then presented his medical diagnosis.

"The smell is within limits," he pronounced as he took another spoonful and proclaimed, "It's edible," all the while looking over at Mary, who was chambering a round in her FN 7.5 handgun while looking at him, just in case there was a question about the cooking.

The doctor then said, "It's delicious. Go for it," while watching Mary, the cook, put the safety on her gun and slip it back into its holster. After a great meal and dessert consisting of key lime pie and water, the guards set their watch schedule. While the team discussed how to proceed in the morning, the hot food and fatigue caught up with everybody, who suddenly got very tired. They decided to turn in, and soon the quiet of the outdoors was broken with an incredible variety of snores.

The next morning, as the group was having breakfast, a battered pickup with a camper top pulled up, and a man and woman got out. They were dressed for the outdoors with jeans, boots, and hats. When one of the guards approached them, they showed some credentials, resulting in a quick trip to the campsite and a private meeting with Dr. Kafka. After about one-half hour, Dr. Kafka approached the group and introduced his "guests."

"Dr. Brown is an expert on alien technology."

"What!" exclaimed Bill. "Alien technology?"

"Yes," said Dr. Brown.

"I had the chance to try to examine," he paused and looked at Dr. Kafka, "what are their clearances?"

"Don't worry. Theirs is higher than yours," said Dr. Kafka.

Why me?

"You don't say," said Dr. Brown, looking at each member of the team.

"Okay, as I said, I got to examine some very interesting 'stuff' at an air base near here called Groom Lake."

"What stuff?" asked Corky.

"I don't want to bore you with a bunch of dull engineering stuff and technical jargon," said Brown.

"I'm an engineer," said Martha, who graduated number two in her class in mechanical engineering at the Air Force Academy.

"My interest was higher temperature materials."

"To save time, can we talk about my work later, and you can translate it to your group?" said Dr. Brown.

Dr. Kafka introduced the other person with, "This is Dr. Evans, who is going to be working with our doctor. Her background is exotic biology."

"What does that mean?" said May.

"I like weird bugs and plants. Humans are okay, too," said Dr. Evans, who happened to be an excellent surgeon and respected researcher.

Dr. Kafka said, "Martha, why don't you review the plan for today to bring our guests up to date?"

Martha began, "Goals for today are to photograph everything and check for any biological or radiation hazards. If safe, try to get the doors open and go from there. We also plan on having lunch and dinner," she added with a look at Dr. K. Dr. Kafka interjected, "Lunch and dinner aren't on the schedule. You all want me to add it?"

A chorus of "yes, hell yes, and amen" followed almost before he finished speaking.

"Okay, I'll add lunch and dinner to the schedule," said Dr. Kafka, chuckling.

"Now, can we stop wasting taxpayer dollars and get moving? Collect your stuff and we'll meet in the main room in 30 minutes."

"Dr. Brown, you team up with Martha. Dr. Evans, you team up with our doctor, okay? Let's get moving."

Chapter 46

The group met inside the reception room exactly 30 minutes later. Fortunately, the room was very large, some 200 feet on each side of its triangular shape. The Brown and Evans teams begin searching for any hazards while the rest of the group begins measuring and photographing everything. Dr. Kafka called a halt for lunch at 1300 hrs. to force everybody to rest and report.

Both Brown and Evans reported that their instruments could not detect anything hazardous, but they stated that there could be something dangerous that they could not measure.

"You mean we could be in danger and not know it," exclaimed Bill.

"Yes," said Martha, "but we could get a bucket of prop wash and cover all exposed areas of your body, and that should protect you from just about anything."

Bill turned to the doctor and asked, "Do you have any?"

"No," said the doctor, "but as soon as the supply helicopter gets here, I'm sure they will have some."

"Great," said Bill.

"Until then, we may not be protected."

"Right," said the doctor.

"But when it comes, you can get it from them."

"Mary," said the doctor, "Do you have a bucket with a lid on it that Bill could keep the prop wash in?"

"Sure do," said Mary, barely able to maintain a straight face.

"When they get here, you can get the bucket from Mary and ask the helicopter crew for some prop wash. I'm sure they will be glad to share some."

"Thanks, Doc," said Bill.

He then got a strange look on his face and said, "Why would I need a bucket for medication?"

The group could no longer contain itself and burst out in a long and loud round of laughter. Finally, Martha took pity on Bill and said, "Prop wash is the wind created from a propeller."

"I get it," said Bill sheepishly.

Bill waited until the laughter died down, turned to the doctor, and said, "Would some hot air work as a substitute? You know, like from a politician," he said turning to look at Dr. Kafka who started turning a light shade of red eliciting another round of laughter from the group.

When it died down, the doctor said, "It might work, but you have to be careful handling it because one needs to know if it comes from a reliable source or from a swamp."

Another round of laughter ensued. Dr. Kafka interjected, "Okay, folks, Comedy Hour's over. How about some honest work, such as finding a way to open those doors?"

Dr. Brown said, "Martha and I have a possible theory that by combining some of the symbols on the keyboard, we might be able to create a symbol that's on the screen."

"I see," said Elaine.

"Let me try this."

"Wait," said Dr. Kafka.

"Let's get ready. First, one person from each team waits outside just in case. Brown and Evans will be in here with Elaine and me."

Most of the group did not want to go out for various reasons, but did go. Corky wasn't very happy and gave Elaine a quick kiss and whispered something in her ear, to which she glared at him and said, "hell, no." He turned and left. Once the team radioed back, they were all outside and clear of the opening.

Dr. Kafka said, "Go." Elaine pressed the first symbol on the keyboard, which represented the first part of the symbol on the board. That part lit up. After the group checked the surroundings, Dr. Kafka gave the okay to press the next keyboard symbol located in the middle of the keyboard. Instantly, the symbol group on the board lit up. She waited until the okay from Dr. Kafka and then pressed the last part of the symbol on the keyboard. The last part lit up on the screen and turned a bright blue. A blue light lit up on the floor going from the desk to one of the doors which slid open, and the frame glowed a bright blue. The two doctors checked the opening for anything coming out that might be harmful while Dr. Kafka and Elaine covered the opening with their sidearms.

With the door open and declared safe, the group paused at the entrance and looked in.

Dr. Kafka said, "Okay, let's send someone in to explore.

"I volunteer, Corky," said Elaine.

Dr. Kafka thought for a minute and agreed. He insisted that May go with him. He then radioed for Corky and May to come back into the reception area. When they returned, Dr. Kafka explained their mission. Corky said,

"Why do you need both of us to go in? I can do it alone. Why do I need her?"

"To protect your dumb ass," piped up Elaine.

Before Corky could reply, Dr. Kafka said, "Enough chit chat. Get moving!"

Chapter 47

The room that Corky and May entered was approximately 50' x 75', oval-shaped, with various niches cut into the stone walls. There was a doorway at the end of the room on the left, and the ceiling was about 15 feet up and studded with those same glow panels. The central area held what looked like tables and chairs arranged in small groups around the room. The room was spotless.

When May approached one of the niches, a voice made a noise, and the niche lit up. May jumped back and looked around for the source of the sound, but there was no one. When she asked Corky if he heard that, he said "no." She tried another niche, and it lit up, and she heard the same sound.

"Corky, you must've heard that."

"No," said Corky.

"If you're hearing things, then you might need some rest or need to see the doctor."

"I'm fine. Come over here and listen carefully," said May.

Why me?

When Corky came within 2 feet, he jumped back, startled.

"I heard that. Is that the sound you were talking about?"

"What sound?" said May.

"I didn't hear anything."

"You're joking," said Corky.

"It was clear as day."

"Wait," said May, and she moved closer to the niche.

"There, I heard it."

"Well, I didn't," said Corky.

"Wait, let me think. If either one of us couldn't hear or the other one could, the sound must be very directional, or it was in our heads. You know, for the second-best fighter on the team (subtly reminding Corky who beat whom in applying for the job to be Tom's bodyguard), I think you might be onto something. Let's test it out. Here, let's try that niche over there," said May, moving toward another niche.

"I just heard a different sound, didn't you?"

"No," said Corky.

"Now I will move back, and you move in. Tell me if you hear anything."

Corky slowly advanced towards the appointed niche. "Now, I just heard it."

"Okay, I didn't, but it looks like when we get within 2 feet is when we hear."

"I'm inclined to agree with you that I think I heard it in my head. If so, it certainly is not any technology I've ever heard of," said May.

"Okay, let's move on. I'm hankering to see what's through that door down there," said Corky, walking toward the doorway at the end of the room.

May followed, still puzzling about what technology could communicate directly to the mind. As they approached, the doorway slid open, revealing a larger room with numerous alcoves cut into the rock wall. In each alcove was a thin foam-like object which, when touched, felt soft. Corky sat down on one of them.

"Wow, this is the most comfortable bed I have ever lain on. You've got to try it."

Why me?

May picked another one and agreed.

"This is way better than my air mattress!"

Then, like a couple of kids testing a new bed, they jumped onto several other bed niches with the same results. They repeatedly heard a different sound in their heads when they were inside the niches.

"I think that's a word or directions," said May as they settled into the oddly shaped chairs to discuss what they had just observed.

"Are you okay, came a voice over their radios."

"We are fine," replied Corky.

"We are in another room through a doorway in the back of the room we went into. Don't know what it is, but it appears safe, so come on in. This room appears to be a sort of dormitory with the most comfortable mattresses you've ever slept on. There's another door, so I will try to see where it goes."

"Be careful, there might be booby-traps or some unknown hazards. Wait for us to check it out," said Dr. Brown.

"Too late," said Corky, moving toward the door, which opened, and suddenly he found himself out in the reception area looking at Dr. Kafka and Drs. Brown and Evans.

"Surprise," said Corky, startling the others.

"It's safe. Why not bring in the rest of the team?"

"Let us check it out first," said Dr. Kafka.

"Okay, but I tell you it's safe. Oh, by the way, don't be surprised if you hear noises in your heads."

"What?" exclaimed Dr. Brown.

"Yeah, we think those are words, but have no idea what they are saying. But don't take our word, just check it out yourselves," said Corky to the backs of Brown and Evans as they rushed through the door.

After about an hour, they reported to Dr. Kafka that it appeared safe for the others to come on in. When Dr. Kafka gave the okay, the charge through the front door looked like a blue light special at Kmart. May and Brown spent about five minutes briefing the group before they all went into the first room.

Chapter 48

While the others explored the room, Elaine spent time exploring the desk. She suspected that bureaucrats in any culture needed some sort of paperwork; otherwise, why have a desk? She tried moving the keyboard to different places, and nothing happened. The small hologram display above the keyboard was still displaying the symbols she had typed in.

Then she started exploring the desk, thankful for the large room, which helped to reduce the noise from the excited jabbering of the various groups exploring the two rooms as she ran her hands over the top of the desk, a compartment opened in one corner. Inside were a number of discs about the size of a silver dollar. She picked one up and turned it around in her hand. She glanced at her keyboard display, and it was now showing the symbols in English.

"What the!" she exclaimed.

Elaine turned to look at the screen behind her. It was now displaying English subtitles next to each group of symbols. One group now reads Dorm, another reads

Substance, another reads Medical, Hanger, Powerplant, and Laboratories.

"Wow, Wow, WOW," exclaimed Elaine.

She was so loud that Dr. Kafka turned to look at her, and for the second time this week, he was shocked to see the screen behind Elaine now in English. He ran over to the desk.

"What did you do? How did you do that?" he yelled.

"I don't know," said Elaine.

"I found a compartment full of these things, and when I picked one up, everything started appearing in English."

By now, the rest of the team had come over to see what the yelling was about, and suddenly everybody started asking questions all at once.

"Quiet," yelled Dr. Kafka.

Once it quieted down, he said, "Now tell me exactly what you did."

"I started searching the desk to see if there was anything else I could find, and when my hand passed over this section, a lid slid back. Inside were all these things. I picked one up, and that's when I noticed the display over the keyboard was in English."

Dr. Brown speculated that there might be some kind of translation device that is activated when you pick it up.

"You sure you didn't do anything else?"

"No, I picked it up and it said What are you?"

"That's it," said Brown.

"It translated into your spoken language. I wonder if they work elsewhere," mused Brown.

"Let's test it," said Corky, grabbing a disc from the pile on the desk.

"I know just the place to try it out." He turned and started jogging towards the room, now marked as the mess hall. Inside, he approached one of the cabinets cut into the rock face.

Now he heard the words "liquids." He then said, "What do you have?" and was rewarded with a very long list of liquids, some in English, and most of the other items apparently didn't have English names. Many sounded like clicks or someone throwing up. By now, other members of the group had gotten their own discs and were trying them out on other niches.

"You've got to see this," said Dr. Evans.

"This section said protein. I asked it to list, and it asked what planet? I said earth, and it rattled out a whole bunch of meat dishes, including hamburger, steak, cod, catfish, lamb, etc. I said, 'I wish I had a hamburger,' and a drawer popped open with a frozen hamburger in it. When I set it on top of the cabinet, it said, 'What temperature?' I said 150°F. In five seconds, the burger was done."

"Don't eat that until it's tested," warned Brown, who had been standing in the middle of the room with Dr. Kafka, trying to monitor the various members of the group.

"I did, and I couldn't detect any pathogens or other harmful organisms," said Evans.

"How did you do that? I don't see any instruments," said Brown.

"I took a careful bite. It was delicious."

"Are you crazy!" shouted Brown.

Why me?

"Well, just keep me under observation for the next few days and see what, if anything, happens to me," retorted Evans. Corky went back to the liquid dispenser and asked for water.

A drawer opened, and an 8-ounce plastic-like glass of water was inside. When he placed it on top of the cabinet, it asked what temperature?

"Let's try 40°F," he said. Within five seconds, the glass was sweating and, when he stuck his finger in it, the water was cold.

After two hours of testing, Dr. Kafka called the group together.

"It's getting near dinnertime. Mary, you and Martha fixed something. We will all, and I mean all, leave our discs here and go out and eat dinner with our guards. Nobody is to say anything about what we discovered here today, or any other day for that matter."

At dinnertime, several of the guardsmen remarked how little some of the usually big eaters in the group were eating. "The docs have got us on some sort of diet to help us adjust to the altitude," said Bill.

After the guardsmen left to begin their duties, the group quietly reviewed their plans for the next day. The docs wanted to check out the med unit. Evans, along with May, would check out the lab sections. Corky wanted to find the Powerplant. Martha wanted to see the hangar along with Tom and Mary. Elaine was to begin documenting what they found out with pictures and journaling.

Once that was settled, they all turned in only to be awakened by the supply helicopter along with the new change of guard. After breakfast, Dr. Kafka briefed the officer in charge of the guards on what their duties were to be. The group then reentered the reception area, picked up their translation discs, and went exploring.

At 1330 hrs. Dr. Kafka ordered the group to get lunch. Later, he would refer to his experience managing this group as trying to herd a pack of cats to do one thing together. Once the group assembled in the alien mess hall and had eaten, Dr. Kafka asked for progress reports. The docs reported that the medical area appeared to have a fairly standard operating area, if you can discount an operating table that could be expanded in any direction. There was a cabinet-like thing with multiple arms that appeared to be some sort of surgical machine.

Why me?

There are many small cabinets containing what appears to be various medications. While the translation disc displayed the names of the ingredients, it didn't give any more information. There were at least five distinct sets of med groups that appeared to be for five different species, including humans. Some of the medications in the human group the doctors recognized, but many of them they didn't. There was a screen in the room that could be some sort of imaging device, but they felt it would take weeks, if not years, to understand everything. They were trying to get it started but were called to lunch. There was a whole lot more in that room that they needed to just look at. But from what little time they had to explore, it would be quite a while before they had any greater understanding of what was available in the med room.

Corky reported that the power room was small and quiet. There was one small structure shaped like a kind of pyramid with a bigger base measuring about 5 feet per side and about 6 feet high. There appeared to be some sort of control panel showing various symbols, for which the translation disc only showed more symbols.

There didn't appear to be any wires, but the top 2 feet of the device kind of glowed. He said he checked for radiation but found none. The machine was making a very faint hum. As to what was causing it, he would need a team of about 100 scientists, engineers, etc., and a couple of years to figure out how the thing worked and what the fuel source was.

May and Doc Evans were next, and both tried to talk at once as fast as a human could talk, trying to tell everything. Dr. Kafka stopped them with a single command, "STOP," which caused everyone to stop what they were doing.

"Slow down, ladies. Most of us can handle one person talking at a time. Dr. Evans, why don't you begin?"

Dr. Jean Evans, Ph.D., opened her mouth and stammered, "I don't even know where to begin. There is a kind of greenhouse with plants I've never seen. There were some plants that appeared to have been found on Earth, but from an earlier time. I've got years of work in just that one area."

Dr. Kafka said, "Thank you," and cut her off as she was starting to gush in some foreign language (Latin) and other words about plants.

"May, you're the physics person in our group. What did you see so far?" said Dr. Kafka.

"So far will pretty well describe it. So far, I have seen sheets of materials that almost float on air but just need some sort of special tool to cut up. There is an instrument that appears to measure the stars."

"What!" exclaimed Joan.

"How did you figure that out?"

"Simple," said May.

"The label on the container said Star Chart. There is other stuff for which I could get multiple Ph.D. D.S. from and probably several Nobel prizes also, if I'm allowed to publish."

"You all remember the nondisclosures that you signed?" interjected Dr. Kafka.

"Nobody talks about anything unless they are cleared by me personally. Are we clear?"

After a chorus of yes, sirs, to keep the rest of the reports moving, he turned to Martha.

"What did your group find out?"

"The hangar is big," said Martha, slowly drawing out the fact that the hangar has half a dozen aircraft or possibly spacecraft in it.

"We haven't accessed any, but they look like they will fly. There is a large fabrication area that looks like it could produce the vehicles we found using something that looks like a huge 3D printer."

"Why hasn't anybody seen or reported this thing?" asked Mary.

"Tom and I think we figured it out. When we moved to explore the opening, there were two hangar-like doors that were open. When I stepped outside, the same holographic projector system made the outside look like the face of the Mesa."

"So, we guess that's why nobody ever noticed a large opening on the face," finished Tom, who suddenly grabbed the sides of his head with both hands and would've fallen off his chair if Corky, who was sitting next to Tom, hadn't grabbed him.

Both doctors rushed over and helped ease him onto the floor. Mary was instantly by his side, stroking his head and asking, "What happened? Is he okay?" while looking at the doctors who started to answer her, but Mary cut in.

"He's okay. That's the way he does it when he has a brain dump. Let him rest and get ready to hear and record what comes next."

Since they were in the mess hall, they helped Tom into the next room, which was the dormitory, and let him lie down in one of the niches. Mary continued to stroke his head while May and the doctors all watched him very closely. After about an hour, Tom sat up, drank a glass of water, and leaned back. He said he was fine, but it would be a bit before he could relate what he had just dumped. After a short while,

Tom's eyes glazed over, and May said, "He's getting ready to dump. Elaine, do you have your recorder ready? Are there fresh batteries because his dumps can be long?"

"Yes, I've got extra batteries and chips," replied Elaine as just then Tom began to speak, and Elaine just barely got the recorder going. What ensued was the group listening for the next six hours, with Tom stopping briefly to drink some water.

At the end of this "short" dump, he said, "I need to sleep," turned over, and started snoring. The rest of the group just sat around with their mouths open, trying to understand what they had heard.

Elaine turned to May and asked, "Is this a normal thing? Usually, he's hooked up to a machine that handles the dump much faster. But actually, this was a small dump compared to what he produced in the past."

Corky said, "I don't understand at least half of what he said. What did it mean?"

"I'll need to get those chips to someone who can translate them," said Dr. Kafka, placing the memory chips from Elaine's camcorder into a small box and walking outside.

With nothing else to do, the rest of the group, except Mary, who stayed to keep an eye on Tom, went to continue their explorations.

Several hours later, Tom was awakened by the sound of a very loud helicopter. He started to get up, but Mary made him lie back down and continue resting.

"What's all the noise?" said Tom.

"Stay here and I'll go see," said Mary, standing up and walking to the door.

Why me?

A few minutes later, she returned and said, "It was one of those planes that can be a helicopter or a plane, you know, the ones that we would occasionally see around the Ontario airport."

"Oh, you mean a Chinook," said Tom.

Dr. Kafka called the group together just before he left and told them that Dr. Brown would be in charge of the scientific side of the group. May and Mary were to manage Tom.

Bill and Martha were to be in charge of any military action, whereas Martha looked at Bill and said, "A Mexican driver in charge of military actions?"

Bill looked at her and said, "You mean an airplane driver who couldn't see what they were bombing is going to tell a special forces Ranger Lieutenant Colonel how to run a ground battle?"

Dr. Kafka broke in and said, "May I introduce Lieutenant Colonel William Gonzales Smith, U.S. Army retired, to Major Martha Jefferson, U.S. Air Force retired. Major Smith has a Silver Star, a Bronze Star, and a Purple Heart. Major Jefferson was number two at the Air Force Academy, the first woman B-52 pilot to fly combat missions.

She has twenty-two combat missions and was in line to be an astronaut until an airplane crash in which she pulled three people from the flaming wreckage that left her injured and disqualified from astronaut training."

At this point, both Martha and Bill looked at each other with an elevated degree of respect. Dr. Kafka then said, "The day-to-day operation will be jointly under Corky and Elaine, who will report to me every 24 hours the daily progress. Anything else?

"No. Back soon." With that, Dr. Kafka turned around and walked to the waiting helicopter.

"Well," said Corky, "It looks like we are on our own for a while, so let's take advantage of the time and try to find out as much as we can. Any questions?"

"Just one," said Brown.

"How do you want our findings to be reported?"

"Well," said Corky, "Mary has been doing journaling and photos, so why doesn't each area plan on a specific time for her to come by and you update your progress?"

"Kinda like they do in Star Trek, but what star date do you want us to use?" quipped Elaine.

Why me?

"Are you really going into TV withdrawal?" asked Corky.

"Maybe the docs have something to help."

"We might have something, but we will need access to the internet connection the guard lets us use. I will need to request a specialized piece of equipment. If you think it will help, order what you need. We need to have all of our members fully functioning, and besides, Dr. Kafka is paying for it."

The doctor began scribbling on a prescription pad, then tore it off and handed it to Corky, who took a look at it and very solemnly looked around the group.

"We will have to vote on this because it may impact all of us," he said.

"Well, let's hear it," said May.

"Okay," said Corky, "do we want a 60- or 70-inch TV?" It took a minute before the group caught on, and then they all started laughing, breaking the tension of the moment. "Okay," said Elaine, "let's get to the fun part of our jobs and get back to work. I'll be around to see you. What's a good time to get with you for your daily reports? You will have to keep them under half an hour, so just give me a summary. The detailed parts should be put in your logs. Any questions? Good, let's go then."

At that point, the group broke up and got to work. Corky turned to Elaine.

"Can you figure out some way to feed these animals without having them stop work to eat, because I know they would resent it?"

"How about one team member takes a 15-to-20-minute break to come to the mess hall, eat something, and then either relieve the other person or take something back?" suggested Elaine.

"Great idea. Why don't you pass the word when you see us for our progress report?"

"Okay," said Elaine, turning to her computer to work out the schedules.

Chapter 49

The group settled into a routine with Elaine pulling the daily team reports into a comprehensive summary and Corky transmitting them over a secure line using the special encryption program on Elaine's computer.

After four days, Dr. Kafka returned at night, flying in a black stealth helicopter that flew directly into the hangar. Martha and Tom had managed to turn off the hologram project so that the pilot could see where to land, and then turned it back on.

Dr. Kafka exited, followed by three other persons. Corky said, "Welcome back. What's happening?"

"Well," said Dr. Kafka, "about half of the DARPA is trying to keep from wetting their pants based on what little has been released to them. They don't know where the information was coming from, but many are burning up IOUs trying to find out. These three nameless gentlemen are from the airbase at Groom Lake, which has another name. It's called Area 51."

"I've heard about Area 51, but I thought it was just a false lead to give the saucer freaks something to talk about," said Corky.

"Oh, it's real," said Dr. Kafka, "and they do more than talk about flying saucers and aliens, which is why these three gentlemen are here. They want to inspect the three saucers in the hangar and see if any could be flown back to Area 51. So, they want to talk to Martha to find out what she thinks since she is a pilot. Also, I need to talk with Tom to discuss his last dump."

Tom's last dump didn't make any sense. Most of it was in a language nobody recognized until Bill suggested they try running some of it by their "rocket translators."

"Who gave you the naming rights?" said Elaine.

"Nobody, I just took it."

"For now, let's just call them translators," interjected Dr. Kafka before a verbal sparring match ignited between Bill and Elaine.

"Okay, okay, but remember, I named it first," said Bill.

Why me?

When Elaine had Tom repeat the "dump," the translator had no problem. But when the team heard the results, they all dropped their jaws and had to sit down. The translator gave them a list of coordinates in a system that nobody recognized. It also gave a name, or so it sounded like a name, after each coordinate. After four minutes, Tom stopped talking. For once, the group was silent. Then Martha spoke up.

"I don't recognize those coordinates. I've had training obviously in celestial navigation because in a B-52, and other flying vehicles that could navigate anywhere in the world, you had to have a way to navigate in case your instruments go out on you. And that has been a growing problem for our astronauts as they go further into space. How do you identify their positions if they are somewhere between the moon and Mars?"

The team went silent for a moment, and then the elephant-in-the-room question was raised by May.

"Tom, this data was implanted in you sometime in the 60s. Does this mean that some time before that, the U.S. knew or had contact with other races not of this earth?"

"I don't know," said Tom.

"All I got is what you just heard. But as a lifelong science fiction fan, if these are coordinates for other races or planets, then that would mean that the U.S. knew or had contact much earlier than we have been led to believe."

"You mean that all that stuff about the Roswell saucer crash is true!" exclaimed Bill.

"Are we going to be invaded like in the War of the Worlds movies?"

"Calm down, Bill," said Dr. Kafka.

"We'll pass stuff up the line along with your reports from each of your areas. Dr. Evans, would you give us a brief summary of what you have learned so far?"

"I was wondering why there was such a large area devoted to different ecological systems. If those are planets at the coordinates Tom just named, then that would match up with the seven distinct areas we've identified. There is one that appears earthlike, but the plants in it are a more primitive life form from earlier times..."

"You mean that the aliens have been here for a very long time, watching us or doing things to us without our knowledge?" exclaimed Bill, getting visibly agitated and jumping up and down.

"Bill," said Dr. Kafka, "if you don't settle down, you're going to have to wait outside until the briefing is over."

Grumbling, Bill sat down muttering something about, "I need a drink, a strong drink." Doc placed a hand on Bill's shoulder and handed him a cup, saying,

"Your wish is my command."

Bill took a big drink, immediately spitting it out. "It's water. What are you trying to do, poison me?" sputtered Bill.

"No, little one. I'm just helping you to wean yourself off that secret stash you keep nipping at that you bribed the guard troops to supply you with."

"What's this about alcohol?" asked Dr. Kafka.

"I just have it for the doctors in case we need it."

"That's the first time I've heard about it, but why don't you let me keep it, so we don't have to try to find you to get it in case of an emergency," said Jack. "Sure, Doc," said Bill sheepishly.

"Can we finish the briefing?"

"Okay," said Dr. Evans.

"If what Tom said is true, then I would speculate that each area is a kind of park so that the aliens could have an area with a touch of home. I will need about five years to have a definite explanation, assuming I don't bother to eat or sleep even with medicinal help," she said while eyeing Bill, who seemed to squirm down further in his seat.

"May, what has your team found out?" said Dr. Kafka, saving Bill further pain.

"Wow! I don't know where to start, gushed May. There are tools set up that appear to measure or produce things so far beyond my experience. For example, I identified something like an electron microscope, but it appears to be able to look at atomic levels, including showing the various components of atoms, I mean, the electrons, around the nucleus. That's only a little of what that thing can do. It probably can do a whole lot more than just that. Just that one instrument could revolutionize 20 or 30 major industries. Another area had a device that appeared to be a telescope. There was no manual, but it acted like it was linked to a telescope outside of Earth's atmosphere. The resolution is incredible. These are the only two items I have been able to identify. I would like to take another year just to classify some of what the other instruments do, let alone determine what they are capable of. I'm like a kid in a candy shop, except I have no limitation on what I can consume. Wow! Wow! Wow."

"I take it that you are not bored," chuckled Dr. Kafka.

"When I get bored in about three or four years, I'll be sure to let you know," gulped May. Dr. Kafka turned to Martha.

"What have you decided along with your two friends from Area 51?"

"First, they are trying to absorb what they have just heard in this highly classified briefing."

Martha said, glancing at the two men sitting off to one side, furiously whispering to each other. "We are pretty sure we agreed that we need to move at least three of the units that appear to be complete. The question is how? They think that it would take at least three or four heavy-lift choppers to do the job. Of course, with that much noise and activity, it would be pretty hard to have much security. Another idea is that they might be flown out."

"What!" exclaimed Bill.

"Fly an alien flying saucer!"

Dr. Kafka said, "This is your last warning. Calm down, or you are out."

"I'm Mexican. It's in my genes to be excitable."

"Well, calm your genes down. Please continue, Martha," said Dr. Kafka.

"There are several reasons why it would be possible to fly the saucers out," said Martha.

"First, inside the saucer, the controls and instruments seem to be designed for a humanoid form, that is, two legs and two arms. Second, there appears to be a kind of simulator in the maintenance area. Third, those gentlemen have informed me that the U.S. has had several saucers for decades, and we have people trained to fly them. These saucers appear to be more advanced than the ones from Roswell that we have been reverse engineering. The purpose of the other three units is not entirely clear. They appear to have mountings for some type of armament. But nothing is mounted. Also, we're not sure if they are flyable. But the other three are."

"How soon will you be able to move them?" asked Dr. Kafka.

"First, we need some experts to ensure that these things are fully functional. Then we need to train pilots on these new systems. If everything is a go, then we might be able to move them within a month or two."

"So much for keeping this base secret," said Dr. Kafka.

"But that's my job," Dr. K continued.

"I know somebody who might be able to solve this problem if he made it out of our base before it was destroyed. I need to check with Washington before we go any further. All of you keep exploring for the next few days, and let me see what I can do. Elaine, will you put a package of what we have so far together for me?"

"Will do," she replied.

"Since it's getting to be mealtime, let's eat and then get back to work," said Dr. Kafka.

With that, the crosstalk between asking questions and answering kept everyone preoccupied until after their meals.

Meanwhile, Dr. Kafka pulled out his SAT phone and called for the special high-speed chopper that was on standby to pick him up for a trip to the airport, and he requested that a fighter be ready to go when he got to the airport. Once the fighter took off, he should be in Washington in about two hours. His meetings would take place shortly after landing. He requested a secure room for the use of the meeting participants on the base when they landed. Then he would have to wait while various experts analyzed his data. Decisions would then have to be made. After the meetings, he would try to locate John, his security chief, from the ranch.

While Dr. Kafka was waiting for his chopper ride, he watched the efficiency of his "crew." Mary moved among the eating agents like a mother, making sure everybody ate and hydrated. Martha almost choked on food while grilling the two guys between bites about the aircraft at Area 51. She was scribbling notes so fast that Mary stopped her hand by taking away her pen, putting a sandwich in it, and watched Martha take several bites before handing back her pen. Bill was trying to listen in on the conversation about Area 51, but it was so technical that he finally gave up and finished his food. Elaine was furiously typing on a laptop until Mary gently closed it and handed her the untouched plate that Elaine attacked to gobble down as quickly as she could so that she could get back to her computer. Corky had somehow sneaked off and was somewhere in the alien base trying to understand more about this alien wonderland. Dr. Kafka was proud of his selection of Mary as the leader of the group. Her Air Force Academy and operational command experience made it clear she was the right choice.

Dr. K called Bill over and said, "I want you with me when I leave because I need a friendly face and more importantly, a person I can trust."

"You like my face," said Bill. "Don't push your luck," said Dr. K.

"Remember, you were hired for your driving ability, not your looks."

About then, the conversation was interrupted with the arrival of the helicopter, and both men turned toward the landing zone. Mary gave Dr. Kafka a questioning look, to which he simply replied, "Bill's coming with me."

"Okay," said Mary.

"We could do with a little peace and quiet around here."

"I'm not that loud… am I, for a Mexican?" asked Bill.

"You're right," said Mary.

"You're more like my Italian parents, loud, but lovable."

Before Bill could reply, Dr. K gently grabbed his arm and escorted him to the chopper. As the chopper lifted off, Mary said, "Things are going to be harried around here with just one amazing discovery after another."

Chapter 50

The chopper flight was a short 20-minute trip to the local airport. They landed right next to a strange-looking airplane. It seemed to have two seats in tandem and several in the nose. Outside, it resembled an old B-58 bomber that used to be the Air Force's old SAC (Strategic Air Command) first all-jet long-range strategic bomber.

The pilot, who was dressed in civilian clothes, approached them and said, "My command said you need to be somewhere very fast, so they sent this unnamed plane from an unnamed base nearby. Since we don't want to spoil any future surprises for the public by hanging around for too many eyes to report seeing it, please climb in," he said as he directed the two men to a small door and ladder just behind the front nose wheel.

As he was climbing up, Bill said, "I hope the seats are comfortable as I need to catch up on my beauty sleep."

"I don't think you'll have much time for that as our flight time is just under two hours."

"What!" said Bill.

"Two hours from Utah to Washington D.C.?"

"Under two hours," corrected the pilot while making sure each person was strapped in and shown how to eject.

Then he sat down in his seat, strapped in, flicked a few switches, checked his glass panels, started the engines, and lifted off. He didn't need a runway since the plane was VTOL (vertical takeoff and landing) capable. Everyone was pressed hard in their seats as the plane zoomed up, passing Mach 5 as it reached 150,000 feet, where it turned towards D.C. Bill's only comment during the flight was, "I gotta get one of these."

Dr. Kafka replied, "If you can spare 900 million plus and an additional 3 to 400 million for spare parts and maintenance each year, I think I may be able to arrange it."

Bill replied, "I just gotta get one of these. Do they take time payments?" Dr. Kafka only chuckled.

As the pilot predicted, they landed one hour and 40 minutes later at Andrews Air Force Base just outside of Washington, D.C. The trailer that the plane landed on was moved into a small hangar where, after the hangar doors closed, they were allowed to disembark.

Why me?

The pilot asked Dr. Kafka, "Should I keep the meter running, Sir?"

"No, I'm afraid we will be here for a while, so get some rest and chow down for now."

"Yes, sir," said the pilot as he touched a small credit card-looking piece of plastic to a small lighted square on the fuselage, just behind the nose wheel. The access door closed, and then the plane seemed to almost relax.

A VIP car met them by the outside door of the hangar and drove them to the VIP area, where they were given card keys to their rooms and special cell phones that were heavily encrypted and only for use on base. A steward appeared and asked if they wanted something to eat.

"I'll have a small crab, Louie, and the wine of your choice," said Dr. K. Bill asked for steak with fries and a Mexican beer.

"We have six Mexican beers. Do you have a preference?" asked the steward.

"Dos Equis," said Bill.

"Thank you," said the steward and left. Less than five minutes later, he was back with the coldest bottle of beer Bill had ever tasted. The food came about 15 minutes later and was perfect.

"I definitely need to go on more trips with you like this," said Bill as he stuffed another piece of the most tender, juicy steak he had had in quite some time into his mouth.

"Enjoy it while you can," said Dr. K, "as the rest of the time we are here, you probably will be lucky to get a sandwich and a bottle of water. Also, don't expect to get a whole lot of sleep either. Right now, as we speak, there are dozens of people pulling in every political favor they can to get in line to talk with us and wanting to know what we have learned. They will also be trying to figure out some way to go back with us," said Dr. Kafka.

"In fact, you ought to be thankful that I'm such a compassionate employer that I told everybody we would arrive tomorrow to allow us a little time to eat, drink, and rest before the inquisition begins."

"If it would help," replied Bill, "I can stay here and hold down the fort in case anything comes up, thereby reducing the pressure on you worrying about what is going on back at the base."

"Oh, no, my friend," said Dr. K.

Why me?

"We're a package deal. You will be right there answering questions about the many things you were pretending you didn't understand while talking to the guys and gals back at the base. You don't want me to think that the U.S. government wasted all that money paying for your advanced degree in engineering, do you? So, after we eat, you need to get some rest, by yourself, to endure what will be coming in the next days."

"Boss, you take the fun out of life," moaned Bill.

After they finished the dinner and the chocolate cream pie for dessert, both men spent some time strategizing about the next day and then went to their rooms (suites) to catch up on some much-needed rest in preparation for the next day's madhouse.

The next morning, the men were awakened in time to have a wonderful breakfast consisting of eggs for Bill and blintzes covered with blueberries for Dr. Kafka. This repast was accompanied by a delicious, strong Colombian coffee available by the gallon. They found, after eating, that a set of clothing had been laid out in their exact sizes in dark colored suits and matching ties. The shoes seem to mold themselves to each man's foot. They were each given an expensive-looking watch that matched their outfits.

"Why do I need another watch?" asked Bill.

"I've got a very good one."

"Please hand over your personal watch," asked the steward.

"They will return it when you are ready to leave."

Dr. Kafka added, "These watches allow somebody to continuously monitor all our vital signs and locations."

"Don't our cell phones have that capability?" asked Bill.

"Yes," said Dr. K.

"But this is the military, and they like to make things in redundancy, so enjoy your watch and let's go."

The two men went downstairs, got into the VIP limo, and drove about a mile, where they stopped in front of a nondescript-looking building and were told by the driver to go on inside as they were expected.

Just inside the front door, they entered a foyer where a Captain sat at a simple military desk with two heavily armed MPs who looked like they were very anxious to use their weapons on the two men. After checking both their palm prints and retinal scans, the Captain reluctantly confirmed their identities.

The MPs then escorted the two men into another room where they were told to wait. Fortunately, there were several comfortable chairs in the room. As the two men sat down, the MPs closed the door, and for 30 seconds, nothing happened. Then the room moved downward several hundred feet, where a young sailor then escorted the two men to a kind of train and showed them seats and told them to strap in. After confirming both men were strapped in, the young sailor stepped out and pressed a button. The hatch closed, and suddenly the capsule started accelerating faster and faster, but there was no sense of movement beyond the initial acceleration. Since there were no visual references outside of the enclosed compartment, there was no sense of motion.

"What's going on?" questioned Bill.

"You, my friend, are being made privy to something suspected by many but known and used by few who travel around this country in this special underground high-speed railway. Our destination was programmed into the capsule's computer and is unknown to the passengers. Eventually, this thing will stop, and we will get out, and then the fun will begin," said Dr. K.

"How fast do you think we are going?" asked Bill.

"Only about 600 miles an hour," said Dr. K.

"No way. If we are underground in a tunnel, the pressure wave being pushed in front of us would be building up too fast for us to go very fast."

"It would be a problem if we weren't in a vacuum on a magnetic levitation system," was all that Dr. Kafka said, looking at Bill, whose eyes could not have opened any wider.

After about 20 minutes, the capsule could be felt to be slowing down. Bill finally regained his voice and muttered, "600 miles an hour is 10 miles a minute times 20 minutes puts us about 200 miles from where we got on this thing. That would put us…"

"Stop!" said Dr. K.

"Any further thought could cause you some serious conversations with the security people. We just had a nice ride, and we have arrived somewhere to face a whole bunch of very excited people."

When they opened the capsule, the two men were greeted by so much brass that Bill thought the floor had to

Why me?

be reinforced concrete to support the weight on the shoulders
of the three people greeting them.

Chapter 51

As Dr. Kafka and Bill got off the tube, the senior ranking General, Clyde Thompson, stepped forward and shook Dr. K's hand.

"Dr. Kafka, you have no idea the massive amount of chaos your preliminary reports have caused among those allowed access to them. General Bernard here of the Space Force has suddenly had the number of sightings of flying objects reported to his command increase dramatically."

Dr. K stepped forward to shake the General's hand.

"Were any of the additional sightings verified?" asked Dr. K.

"Many were older sightings that people suddenly felt freer to report. So far, most of the sightings haven't been authenticated."

Gen. Thompson interrupted, "Admiral Smith here has been almost heroically trying to keep the Navy under some control."

Dr. K stepped over and shook Adm. Smith's hand, then said, "I imagine that trying to keep those young hotshot pilots under control is like trying to control shoppers at a blue light Kmart special."

"If it were that easy, it would be no problem," replied the Admiral.

"How do you keep your herd of scientists from spilling the beans? Several of them are well-known in their fields and haven't been heard from in a while. Some people in the science community are starting to ask questions."

"I try to keep them so busy that they have trouble trying to eat and sleep," replied Dr. Kafka.

"I expected to see the Air Force represented in this group. Where is he?"

General Thompson (Chairman of the Joint Chiefs of Staff) replied, "General Bernard lost the toss and is trying to keep the crowd inside from engulfing you.

Then, turning to Bill, said, "I'm sorry, we haven't been introduced. I'm General Bernard."

"Lieutenant Colonel retired Bill Hernandez," filled in Dr. Kafka.

In turn, Bill snapped a perfect military Academy salute that was formally returned by General Thompson, the ranking officer.

General Thompson then said, "We better go and meet the inquisition before they overrun General Bernard."

The group then entered through the doors on the platform into a large room with half a dozen MPs from all branches of the services. Another group of MPs was in special enclosures with remote-controlled weapons, including two lasers, noted Dr. Kafka, as they swept through the room and out a nondescript door in the back of the room.

Upon barely entering, the group was immediately bombarded with, "About time. Do you know how long you have kept me waiting?" Or "How soon can you get me to Site Gamma?"

Bill leaned over and quietly said, "Site Gamma?" to Dr. Kafka, who responded, "I'll explain later."

The two were escorted to the podium, where Bill, who was a certified hero, nervously started looking for a way out of this madhouse of roughly 60 people all trying to talk at once over each other. As the generals returned to their seats in front, General Thompson stepped to the podium microphone and gave several loud hits on the mic, causing a very loud bang that got those in attendance to sit down.

As all quieted down, he said, "Today's agenda will be simple. Dr. Kafka will present his latest discoveries. Then we will have lunch provided by the Navy. Afterward, Dr. Kafka and his aide will attempt to answer as many written questions using only the pads on your desks. No shouted questions will be answered, only written ones. Also, be sure you include your name and affiliation, or your questions will not be addressed. Any person disrupting these proceedings will be removed by the MPs and held in another room where they can listen but will have no contact with the speakers. Since there are no procedural questions, we will proceed," said the General, ignoring several hands that were immediately raised. Dr. K calmly stood up and began clicking for the first slide.

He began, "As you know, on September 11, a group of terrorists managed to attack one side of the Pentagon. What was not known was that in the rebuilding process, a hidden and unknown room was discovered. In that room was a simple safe (showing slide of the safe). In that safe was a set of documents referring to a base you now call Site Gamma. Based on that limited information contained in those documents, the Joint Chiefs commissioned me to locate the site. After considerable effort on the part of my team members, including retrieving information from an almost forgotten data storage program, a terrorist group somehow gained access to our itinerary, resulting in several encounters with loss of life on both sides. However, we now fully control the site, thanks to the Utah National Guard. He then showed a slide of the National Guard soldiers holding several prisoners. Upon limited investigation of the site, we have discovered the following."

Dr. Kafka then began with a slide show explaining what the team had found during the brief time available to his team, along with the speculation of the possible functions of various components within the site. After 90 minutes, the audience was so stunned that one could literally hear a pin drop on the carpeted floor. Then a murmur started and swelled into a roar, mostly composed of words like "Unbelievable, impossible, what the hell," etc.

General Thompson stepped up to the mic and said, "Thank you, Dr. Kafka. You have given us much to think about during lunch. Our written questions will be ready for you after lunch. This meeting is adjourned until 1400 hrs. You all know where the mess hall is, so dismissed."

Why me?

"Dr. K and Bill, if you will follow me, we have a quieter place to eat," said the General, turning to lead them out a side exit before they could be waylaid by people expecting to receive special access to them.

During lunch in the executive dining room, Bill and Dr. K were basically left alone, excluding the four very serious MPs guarding access to the team. The exception was a female Marine Sgt. who came in pushing a hand truck holding a large plastic box filled with yellow note sheets.

Looking at the mountain of questions, Bill said, "The group had that many questions?"

"This is only part. There is at least another box full to be brought in," replied the Sgt.

Dr. K said, "Bill, now is the time for you to earn your keep. Sort out these questions into two stacks. One stack that is legible and one that isn't. The ones we cannot read will be returned to the author to be legibly rewritten. After that initial sorting, we will then sort the questions into various categories. We should finish this just in time for our next meeting. While I'm answering these questions, you can be sorting through the next box, eliminating questions we have already answered."

"You want me to sort and answer questions at the same time?" exclaimed Bill.

"You didn't do anything this morning, so you need to catch up by doubling up," was the reply. Bill asked, "Why are we returning the notes instead of asking the person whose name is on them to ask their question verbally?"

"Because that's a trick to allow the person to ask questions that may not be on their note thereby hogging the Q&A time," said Dr. K.

They had barely finished when the General came in to escort them back to the meeting. They gave the illegible notes to his aide to be returned to the authors for rewrite. When Bill and Dr. K had entered the hall, it was as if a plug was pulled, and the hall became very quiet except for the scratching of opinions on paper. Bill was given a table to sit at on stage, along with a microphone. Dr. K sat at another table with a microphone and dramatically started reading and answering the questions.

Most of his answers were, "This is what we think that is or think that is its function."

He tried to show pictures of the device or area that pertained to the question. Occasionally, he asked Bill for his assessment of the question. After three hours, Dr. K had gone through two-thirds of the legible questions. The meeting was then adjourned until nine hours the next day. Bill and Dr. K then rode the tube back to the base to eat, rest, and plan the next day. The next morning, they boarded the tube at eight and a half hours to begin the same routine of Q & A, lunch, Q & A, home, repeat the next day.

After three days, all of the questions from the first day's set were answered. The deeper probing questions would be answered after Dr. Kafka consulted with the team at Site Delta.

After four days, Bill and Dr. K were allowed to return to the site "to get answers" to the follow-up questions.

When Bill and Dr. K return to the site that night, they are flown into the mountain without lights. Bill almost had a heart attack when he saw the nose of the very quiet and stealthy helicopter seemingly going to crash into the side of the mountain.

"Relax. The pilot is using infrared to guide us in, plus we are being brought in by remote control," Dr. K said as the helicopter appeared to encounter the mountain wall.

When Bill opened his eyes, they were landing inside the big hangar. Martha met them and escorted them to the mess hall, where she gave them a very comprehensive report of what had been accomplished during the last four days.

"This place is even more incredible. To save time, the team has moved completely into the complex. The docs have declared all the food for humans dispensed in here to be safe and probably healthier than what we have been eating on the outside."

Bill groaned, "What kind of healthy food? You mean all sorts of vegetables and other weird stuff?"

"No," replied Martha. "Let me show you what I mean."

With that, she walked to a niche with a crudely labeled sign proclaiming meats and ordered an 8-ounce New York strip steak at 130°F, grilled top and bottom, with a side of French fries. Three minutes later, a door opened, and inside was a perfectly prepared New York strip steak with the best French fries one could hope for.

She gave Bill a knife and fork and said, "Go for it." Bill picked up the serving dish and inspected the steak from all sides.

Why me?

He said, "It looks and smells like a steak."

"Go ahead, taste it," said Martha.

Reluctantly, Bill cut off a small piece, looked at it, and smelled it carefully. Then he finally put it in his mouth and his eyes jumped open while he very thoughtfully chewed the sample.

He gushed, "That is the finest steak I have ever tasted. It's more tender and tastier than the finest Kobe beef I've ever had." He then sampled the French fries.

"Perfect, crisp on the outside, cooked on the inside, and the flavor is wonderful," he gushed while trying to stuff more food into his mouth.

Laughing, Martha said, "The resident cooks were jealous until they found out that the food niches could make food from scratch. Once a recipe is entered and approved, the system remembers it. So now people have been loading in their favorite recipes from home."

"What about wine and other 'adult drinks,'" asked Dr. K.

"That's where this system's ability to learn takes place. See that small grid-like structure in front of the doors of each food niche? If you insert a sample and add a name, the system will reproduce it exactly. Here, try this," she said, walking over to a niche labeled liquids and saying, "A 6-ounce Rhein 2022 vintage, 55°F."

Three minutes later, a door opened and a glasslike cup appeared. "Here, taste it," said Martha, handing Dr. K the glass. Dr. K looked at it, smelled it, then tasted it.

"This is wonderful," he exclaimed.

"Okay, that is great," said Bill, thinking about other samples he would introduce that were not wine.

"But what is all of this made from?"

"That's the kicker," said Martha.

"Several of the scientists are trying to solve that question, but haven't reached a conclusion. One idea is that all of the devices that yield or produce something might be using basic hydrogen atoms from the surroundings, including the atmosphere, and combining those atoms to create anything you want."

"That's impossible," stammered Bill.

Why me?

"You've come to the right place. Welcome to Impossible Island," laughed Martha.

For the next two weeks, the team members settled down into learning more about their area of specialty. Additional experts were brought in and, before they were turned loose, they were given a thorough orientation by Mary, who also submitted a comprehensive report of progress every five days. Each report generated more requests for additional information or to be allowed to visit the site.

A sample of the more useful items found in her reports was from Dr. Jean Evans, who identified a compound that appeared to be able to dramatically increase the growth of any targeted plant. She speculated that this alone could eliminate world hunger. Corky found a small object measuring 6" x 6" x 2" that turned out to be a battery in one of the saucer-like machines in the hangar. What was so unique was that the battery could power a saucer from the base to anywhere on Earth and return on one charge, and it could be recharged in 20 to 30 minutes just by placing it next to a power source. Corky speculated that the battery could probably eliminate fossil fuels if we could figure out how it worked and how to reproduce it. Both medical doctors had to be forced to eat and sleep because they were so engaged in categorizing the equipment and solutions in the medical suite. As discoveries were made and results were sent to various labs around the country for further study, more and more questions were raised from the outside labs as to the source of the material.

Dr. Kafka carefully controlled the release of those items so as not to alert foreign interests as to their source. Meanwhile, Martha had spent every working hour (and some hours when she was supposed to be resting) in the simulator. She described the simulator as being nothing she had ever used or even heard about from DARPA contractors.

"You get in, sit down, and put on the helmet, which seemed to adjust automatically to your head."

She noted it took two days to fit a helmet to a pilot in order to fly an F-35. This thing did it in seconds. Suddenly, she could see and feel the controls and instruments labeled in English as she was walked through basic flying skills. The simulator would not let her move on until she mastered each lesson at the 100% level. She believed she would soon be ready to fly one saucer to Area 51. Before that, she would have to wait until sign off by everybody who was in government or thought they were God, or so it seemed.

Why me?

The team meeting was held every two days to discuss the progress of the various teams and what to do next. Meanwhile, the terrorists had been mostly forgotten. However, they were not forgotten by Dr. Kafka. He was able to locate John, his previous head of security at the hacienda, to take over the security at the site. The change was like night and day. All the findings of each team were compartmentalized and released only with Dr. Kafka's approval. John arranged to have several homestead-like areas, complete with cabins, built in different locations around the immediate area.

The families who occupied these cabins were actually very highly trained operators who were rotated in and out on a random schedule. Electronic surveillance was hidden using the same technology that the team first discovered when Tom fell through the rock. Tom finally got the equipment to record his random dumps, which freed up May to help Mary keep up with the reports from the teams. The pilot who helped the team during the battle was recovering in a VIP retreat. A fake burial was done with coverage in the local newspaper to protect him from terrorist retaliation for what he had done for the team. The terrorist boss, Mohammed, was actually in attendance as one of the funeral drivers for the closed-casket burial. Due to the security measures John imposed, Mohammed could not get close to Site Delta, but after observing the level of security, he knew he had to find out what was there. So, he started planning his return.

Chapter 52

At Site Delta, things got a bit more exciting in the fourth week when Martha was finally cleared to move from the simulator to the real thing. But, at first, she was only allowed to hover within the hangar. The original team was the only people allowed to observe her first flight. Otherwise, there would have been a riot among team members. Everybody else was moved to other sections of the complex for safety's sake. After 20 minutes, Martha set the saucer down exactly where she had taken it off.

As the team congratulated her, she said anyone could learn to fly these things because there was no discernible difference between the simulator and actually flying the real thing. The next step involved flying the three working units to area 52, not 51. This would be done at night, even though each ship had some sort of cloaking system. These things were so quiet that the normal noise of the generators that the National Guard used for power would cover the takeoffs. It was decided that, as soon as the other pilots arrived and had checked out in the simulator and received Martha's clearance, the ships would leave.

The new pilots were both test and combat pilots. As such, they were ready in six days, and on the night of the seventh day, they all left for Area 52. On the night they were scheduled to leave, Dr. Kafka called Martha to a private meeting to say goodbye.

"Martha, are you confident you and the others will be able to get those things over to area 52?" asked Dr. K.

"About as much as one can be without 18 months of training, 46 manuals to study, and hundreds of hours of classroom instruction by a well-trained support staff and at least a gazillion hours of training in the simulators. Yes, we are ready," replied Martha with a huge smile.

"Then go, Gal," said Dr. Kafka, shaking her hand.

She felt something pass from his hand to hers, and when she looked down, she saw it was a challenge coin, both unique in design and weight.

When she looked up, Dr. Kafka said, "Yes, it's solid gold and you have earned it from your second day working for me. Since you will be away for at least six months, I didn't want you to forget us."

Why me?

Martha looked up at Dr. Kafka with her eyes beginning to mist, but not tearing because Colonels do not cry. Martha remembered when Dr. K found her. Mostly a broken person with a silver star who would have been awarded the Congressional Medal of Honor but couldn't have the publicity that accompanied the medal. She had saved several hundred people by flying an unauthorized mission in a "borrowed" C-130 from a semi-dry rice paddy under heavy fire from an unnamed country to the safety of an American base three hours away.

And, yes, there could be no mention of the Purple Heart she received from being hit in the leg with a sniper bullet aimed for her head. But because the plane was taking off, the bullet hit her leg instead. The pain was excruciating, but she stopped the bleeding by stuffing a roll of bleeding stop gauze into the wound. After she landed the plane at the base, she passed out from the loss of blood. When she awoke four days later, she got the information that her copilot and another crewman had died, and many of the passengers had wounds but would recover.

Two children would not. And, since she disobeyed orders and took the plane into the rice paddy, she would not be flying anymore. The pain of the wound, the losses of the two close crewmen who were like family, the deaths of the two children, and the loss of flying status drove her into depression. She acted out against anybody around her, desperately trying not to ever grow attached to another human being again.

That's when Dr. Kafka showed up, looked her eye-to-eye and said, "I've got a job. If you take it, you will need to forget any friends you ever had. You will have to move somewhere in the Southwest, so hope you don't sunburn easily. The pay is pretty good, but you will have to prove you are as good as you think you are. You will retain your rank and privileges, but you will be a glorified gofer and, if you're any good, you will have the ride of your life. You will work directly for me and, if you agree, you'll have to stop feeling sorry for yourself. Let me make this clear. People often die in wars. You didn't. If you agree, I will work your ass off and tolerate no less than 110%. Am I clear? Any questions?"

Martha looked him in the eye and said, "Yes, Sir, when do I start?"

"Five minutes ago. Here are your orders," said Gen.

Kafka pulled one folded paper and an envelope from his coat pocket. "Wheels up in one hour, Colonel."

Why me?

"How the hell did he know I would accept?" she thought as she stepped back three feet and gave Dr. Kafka an Academy-level salute and said, "See you, Sir." Dr. Kafka matched her salute as only an active Air Force two-star General could and said, "Carry on."

He turned around and left, hiding a sudden misting in his eyes, no doubt from the dry air. Martha read the first sheet assigning her to something called Red Cloud, along with her flight assignment that left in 59 minutes from now. She opened the envelope, and her eyes widened. Shades of SAC (The old Strategic Air Command). The paper informed her that she was now a full Colonel with all the privileges of rank. Then two little silver eagles fell out of the envelope. This followed the old tradition of SAC that, if accepted into SAC, you are automatically promoted one grade. "What have I gotten into?" Martha thought as she hefted the challenge coin for a bit, put it back into her pocket, and went to pilot a flying saucer.

When Martha got to the hangar, it turned out that the rest of the crew was there to send her off with handshakes and hugs. Martha didn't realize how close they had become over the last year, and that led to a warm feeling she hadn't had since her mission in the C-130. She did her preflight checklist. She next checked in with the other two pilots. They then took off into the night, each pilot in a real damn flying saucer!

As Martha left the hangar bay, the crew heard a voice.

"Okay, she's left. Now you can stop wasting taxpayer money and get back to work."

"Slave driver," muttered Bill.

"Thank God that is the only way you get any work done," said Mary, turning around and running away before Bill could retaliate, causing a general round of laughter as all returned to their respective jobs.

After takeoff from the mountain, Martha settled into the routine of sitting back (a little) and just watching the instruments since the flight was basically autopilot-controlled. You just set it, push the green button, and off it goes automatically selecting the speed and altitude, plus it activates some sort of cloaking device. About the only thing for the pilot to do was to sit back and read a book, so she thought, when one small corner of the main screen started blinking purple.

Why me?

"What's that for?" thought Martha. According to the simulator, that was a communication notification. But we were using our own American-made radios.

However, she decided to check in with the other two saucers and, yes, they had the same purple flashing light. What should they do?

"Don't do anything. We should be arriving in 15 minutes. Let's talk about it on the ground."

The light changed to orange, and a gravelly voice uttered something in a number of strange sounds, kind of like a cross between a dog whining and a cat hissing.

"Oh, crap, what now?" thought Martha as she clicked on her radio.

"Are you guys getting this?" said Martha. As she was talking, the light turned blue.

"Are you human?" asked the same gravelly voice.

Martha thought about not answering, but curiosity got the better of her and she replied, "Yes, who are you?"

The voice stopped, and she heard what could be called a major catfight going on in the background.

9 781966 642602